BETWEEN YOUR HEART AND MINE

A NOVEL

BUCK TURNER

INTRODUCTION

Thank you for purchasing this book. To sign up for my newsletter, or to join my team of beta readers, please sign up on my website at:

www.buckturner.com

PROLOGUE

SOMETIMES GOOD THINGS FALL APART SO BETTER THINGS CAN FALL together.
—Marilyn Monroe

CHAPTER 1

A Good Deed

"That'll be four fifty." Joyce Mahan handed a caramel latte to a whisper of a man in skinny jeans. He produced his debit card and slid it through the card reader, keeping his eyes glued to the machine until it flashed Approved. When the transaction was complete, Joyce watched in amusement as he slipped quietly into the side room, took a seat by the window, and stuffed a pair of EarPods into his ears.

Where have all the real men gone? Joyce mused as she put on a fresh pot of coffee.

Her rhetorical question was answered in less than a heartbeat as the front door swung open and in walked Nick Sullivan, a well-built thirty-eight-year-old with chestnut eyes, long brown hair, and a permanent five-o'clock shadow.

"Morning, Nick." Joyce brushed back the auburn hair from her eyes. She was nearly twenty years his senior, but that didn't stop her from looking.

"Joyce, how's everything this morning?" His Southern drawl was thick enough to bottle.

"Good so far, but it's early." She dropped a fresh batch of doughnuts into the hot oil.

Nick flashed a grin as he leaned against the counter. For as long as he had been frequenting the coffeehouse, Joyce had greeted him the same way, but he never tired of the banter. In fact, he rather enjoyed the familiarity of their exchange.

The Gap Creek Coffeehouse sat at the edge of town, just steps from the railroad tracks. Everyone from Pineville to Powder Springs knew about the place, and most people frequented the little hole-in-the-wall three or four times a week as part of their morning or afternoon routine. The place served coffee of course but also tea, hot chocolate, espresso, and cappuccino. There were even croissants, sandwiches, small bites, and about the best desserts around, all made from scratch.

Given its proximity to the university in the neighboring town of Harrogate, the coffeehouse attracted a rather diverse crowd, so it wasn't uncommon to find students, faculty, and locals alike enjoying afternoons beneath the shade of the giant poplars that dotted the grounds. It was a quiet hangout for anyone who wanted to escape and enjoy the beautiful scenery or listen to the babbling brook that meandered lazily along the edge of the property.

"The usual, I presume?" Joyce reached for the pot of black coffee, which had just finished brewing.

"Actually, I was thinking of trying something different today."

"Be still, my heart." She raised her eyebrows as she turned back to him.

Joyce knew Nick better than most, which wasn't saying much since he didn't allow anyone to get too close. But in the three years they had known one another, she had never once seen him order anything other than black coffee.

"I guess you *can* teach an old dog new tricks."

He smiled again, broader this time.

"In that case, what can I get you?"

"I'm feeling ambitious today." He rubbed his hands together and perused the blackboard menu above the counter. "How about a hot chocolate? And a bit of whipped cream if it's not too much trouble?"

"Coming right up." She seemed delighted as she went to work steaming the milk. "I've been meaning to ask you how the chickens are coming along—any eggs yet?" she shouted above the whirring of the frother.

"Any day now." He reached for his wallet. "To be honest, I can't wait. The ones from the store aren't bad, but they're not the same as farm eggs."

"You're not kidding." She began mixing in the chocolate. When it was a silky consistency, she spooned a dollop of whipped cream on top, applied the lid, then handed it to him. "That'll be two dollars." She punched the total into the register.

"Fair enough." He plucked a couple of singles from the stack of bills.

"You'll want to let that cool for a minute." She smiled. "Wouldn't want you to scald your tongue."

"Thanks for the warning." When she wasn't looking, he dropped a five into the tip jar, then grabbed a napkin and a mixing straw and turned to leave.

"I don't suppose I could talk you into doing me a favor?"

His hand on the doorknob, Nick stopped and turned back, detecting a hint of desperation in her voice.

"That depends." He grinned, warming his hands around the cup.

"It's just… Sam is in class this morning, and I was counting on him to make the deliveries."

"How many you got?

"Just the one. It's going to the university. The new English professor phoned it in, and I'd hate to make a bad first impression. Things are tight these days, and every dollar counts."

This wasn't the first time Nick had heard her make a comment like that, which wasn't surprising, considering the recent economic downturn. All the local businesses seemed to be suffering, some more than others. Visiting the coffeehouse had become part of his daily routine, not to mention he enjoyed Joyce's company, so the last thing he wanted was for the business to fail, especially if there was something he could do to help.

"All right, if you're gonna twist my arm." He chuckled as he eased back to the counter. "I have to go by there on my way home, so—"

"Anyone ever tell you you're a saint?" She poured the milk.

"Only you." He smiled, then cleared his expression. "This professor got a name?"

"Eve." She looked at the order slip. "She didn't give a last name, but her office is on the top floor of Avery Hall. You know the place, right?"

"I'll find it." Nick was familiar with the university. It had been a while since he was last on campus, but he had been there several times over the years for special events, so he knew his way around.

"Thanks again, Nick. You're a lifesaver." She handed him the cup. "See you tomorrow?"

"Lord willing." He stepped out into the brisk morning air.

Although later than usual, the cool days of fall had finally descended on East Tennessee. Skies of indigo provided the perfect backdrop for an endless sea of hickory, oak, and birch, set ablaze with bursts of golden yellow and burnt orange.

By the time Nick made it to his truck, the sun had risen above the eastern ridge. He placed the cups in the holders, then slid into the seat and started the engine. While he waited for the fog to clear from the windshield, he rubbed his hands together. He didn't much care for the cold, but it wouldn't take long for the engine to heat, so he gave it a few seconds before backing out.

When the fog had cleared and the cab was warm and toasty, he drove to the end of Pinnacle Alley, then hung a right on Brooklyn Street. From there, he passed beneath the railroad trestle and climbed the hill away from town. After a quick trip down the Cumberland Gap Parkway, he made a right onto Robertson Avenue and entered the university, where he parked in the lot behind the academy. He went the rest of the way on foot, taking his time not to spill the drinks.

Avery Hall sat on the east end of the quad and was home to the English and History departments. It occupied the space where the Four Seasons Hotel once stood. Many of the professors kept their offices on the third floor, so rather than risk a disaster on the stairs, Nick found the elevator and pressed the button, then waited patiently for it to take him up. Fortunately, class was still in session, so the hallways were virtually empty save for a handful of students sitting around a coffee table, having a last-minute cram session. He didn't envy them in the least.

When the doors finally opened, he exited onto the third floor and set his eyes upon the directory. After locating the name of Professor Eve Gentry, he found her room number along with an arrow pointing him in the right direction. He turned right and walked to the end of the hall where a door had her name engraved on a gold plate near the top. Although the door was slightly ajar, he gave an obligatory knock before entering, then eased it open with the toe of his boot.

"Miss Gentry?" he whispered, peeking inside.

"Come in," she said without looking up.

To his surprise, Nick entered to find an attractive young woman in a sleeveless white blouse sitting behind a desk. He had never been the best at guessing ages, especially with women, but she appeared to be in her early thirties. Her long dark hair was pulled up into a bun, and she had on a pair of thin-rimmed reading glasses that framed her face beautifully. He watched in silence as she finished highlighting passages from Tom Sawyer to prepare for her morning lecture.

"Can I help you?" She looked up.

For a second, during which Nick's mind was a mix of confusion and wonder, words escaped him. Working against him was the image he had constructed of her in his head on the drive over. He supposed, as he fought to pull his gaze away from her mesmerizing blue-green eyes, he had expected her to be older, or ordinary, or both. Perhaps he needed her to be. But the woman sitting before him was anything but ordinary.

When he'd collected his thoughts, he said, "I... um... hot chocolate." He handed her the drink as a wave of heat crept up the sides of his neck and face. "Joyce, from the coffeehouse, said you called it in this morning." His words apparently did little to erase her confusion. "Sam, the kid that normally delivers for her, is in class this morning, so she asked if I wouldn't mind dropping it off."

"That's odd. I don't remember calling in a hot chocolate."

"Really? I saw the order slip myself." He studied her face as she appeared lost in thought. "I can take it back if you don't want it." There had to have been a mix-up.

"No," she replied quickly. "I'll take it. Anything is better than what they keep in the professor's lounge." She grimaced. "It more closely resembles motor oil than coffee."

He chuckled, then said, "Careful with that. You don't want to burn your tongue." He watched her lift the brim of the cup to her lips.

"Thanks for the warning." She kept her eyes glued to him as she sipped slowly. Immediately, her eyebrows went up. "This is fantastic." She looked pleasantly surprised. "You know what? Now that I think of it, I'll bet this is Cindy's doing. She's my graduate assistant," she explained. "I was telling her the other day about how it's been years since I've had a good cup of hot chocolate."

"Well, there you have it. Mystery solved." He chuckled, feeling a sense of relief.

"So, do you work for…? Help me out."

"Joyce?"

"Yes. Thank you. Joyce."

"No," he replied quickly, careful not to give the wrong impression. "Like I said, she was a little shorthanded this morning. I guess I was just in the right place at the right time."

"That was sweet of you." She smiled as she took another sip. "I'm sorry. Where are my manners? I'm Eve." She stood and presented her hand.

She was taller than he expected, standing five six or seven in heels, but she was still small beside him. Nick was every inch of six two, even without the boots.

"Nick Sullivan." He gave her hand a gentle shake.

"Pleasure to meet you, Nick."

"You as well," he replied.

She set the cup down on her desk and reached for her purse. As she did, Nick's eyes fell to her black pencil skirt, admiring the way it accentuated her curves. *A look won't hurt,* he told himself as he took her in with his eyes. She was slender, athletic, and it was obvious she took care of herself.

"What do I owe you?"

He quickly raised his gaze. "On the house." He laid a hand gently on top of hers. "Like I said, it was on my way."

She lowered her eyes. "Well, thank you," she said.

"You're welcome." He calmly withdrew his hand and took a step back. "So you're new here. How do you like it so far?"

"Huh? Oh... the jury's still out," she said. "I've only been here since summer, but so far, everyone has been extremely nice." She reached over and stuffed her wallet back into her purse. "I was looking for a change of pace, and I definitely got that."

He detected a hint of sarcasm, and before he knew it, a faint smile had begun at the corners of his mouth.

"I take it you're not from the country?" he guessed, having already decided she was a city girl.

She gave a playful smile. "I am, but it's been a long time. I grew up in a small town in east Texas called Athens. Ever heard of it?"

Nick shook his head. The only things he knew about Texas were barbecue, the Alamo, and the Dallas Cowboys.

"Didn't think so," she said, clearly not surprised. "It makes this place look like New York City." She cracked a smile. "I moved out when I was eighteen and lived the past fifteen years in Dallas before moving here."

City girl. Nick did the math in his head. Thirty-three—he was right. He stifled a smile.

"What about you?" she asked, her eyes taking him in from head to toe. "Work jacket, jeans, cowboy boots—you lived here your entire life, or you just dress the part?"

Nick was amused by her impression of him. "No," he confessed. "I'm originally from Virginia, near Roanoke. I moved to the area a few years back, and no, I don't just dress the part." He could expound on his childhood spent working on his parents' farm or that he now had fifty acres, but it seemed like a fruitless endeavor.

She reached for the phone in her back pocket and checked the time. "I hate to be rude, but I've got a class now."

She lifted the strap of the purse onto her shoulder. Taking the briefcase in one hand and the hot chocolate in the other, she awkwardly tried to pick up the stack of books on her desk.

"Let me help with those." Nick tossed his empty cup in the wastebasket, then in a swift motion, scooped up the books in one hand and followed her out into the hall.

"Thanks again," she said as they headed off toward the elevator. "For the hot chocolate and the help with the books."

"My pleasure."

They made small talk while they rode the elevator to the first floor, then exited and turned right. He walked ahead and cleared a path for her through the sea of students. Stopping at the large classroom she'd indicated at the end of the hall, Nick, being a gentleman, opened the door for her.

"I see in this part of the world, chivalry isn't completely dead. Set them anywhere you like."

He laid the books on the table, then slid out of the way as students began filing into the room. "Well, it was nice meeting you," he said, eager to leave.

"Likewise," she replied with a warm smile.

FROM THE DOORWAY, Eve watched Nick make his way quickly toward the exit. He looked tough, but she had seen enough cowboys in her life to know looks could be deceiving. Earlier that summer, when she accepted the job at the university, she had promised herself not to get involved with someone for a very long time.

Then this chivalrous man in boots, jeans, and a tan corduroy jacket appeared in her doorway out of nowhere.

While he had gazed out the window, she had glanced at his hand—no wedding band. *Divorced*, she thought. Impossible that someone who looked the way he did had never been married. Either way, they were in the same boat, she and Nick, as she was a recent divorcée herself.

She had meant her vow to stay away from men with every bit of her damaged heart, but as she stood there thinking about his quiet strength and the unmistakable sadness in his eyes, she had already decided that for the man who brought her hot chocolate, she would gladly make an exception.

CHAPTER 2

SERENDIPITY

For the past three years, Nick had called the town of Sharps Chapel home. Twenty miles south of the university, the quiet hamlet lay miles from the beaten path on the shores of Norris Lake. When Nick and his wife had first moved to the area fourteen years earlier, they settled in Speedwell, which lay on the other side of the ridge, between Harrogate and La Follette. The vast, sprawling Powell Valley, with its grand views of the high bluffs and proximity to the river, had won them over. But after the accident, Nick couldn't stomach the thought of living with all those memories, so he packed up everything he owned and moved closer to the lake.

Since moving to the farm, Nick passed the days by piddling in his workshop or taking care of his horses. But in the evenings, he would sit alone on the shore of the lake and stare out at the water, remembering the life he once knew.

He wasn't independently wealthy, so Nick ran a small tack business out of an old tobacco barn he'd spent two years restoring. He had grown up around horses, and no one knew the business better than him when it came to riding gear, grooming equipment, blankets, and feed. His special area of expertise was restoring old saddles, a skill he'd gained while spending countless hours as a teenager working on his grandfather's horse farm.

By the time Nick returned home, he was surprised that the professor was still on his mind. It was a thirty-five-minute drive from the university to his farm, so there had been ample opportunity for his mind to wander. And yet, as he parked the truck and cut the engine, there she was.

He set off for the chicken coup and considered why Eve had not left his thoughts. She had the looks, but it was more than that. Even in their brief meeting, he could sense both her wit and intelligence, not to mention her confidence. It had been many years since a woman had impressed him, but as he reached the gate, there was little doubt in his mind Eve Gentry was no ordinary woman.

When he'd fed the chickens, Nick made his way up the hill to the two-story farmhouse he'd restored with his own two hands. Once inside, he glanced at the photograph on the mantel and said hello to his wife and daughter, then checked the messages on his machine. He wasn't fond of cell phones, so he relied on an answering machine that sat on the counter between the living room and kitchen.

The red light on the display told him he had two new messages. One was from Henry Brooks, a local farmer looking for a blanket for one of his horses, and the other was from a woman named Marjorie Cantrell, a longtime client from Maynardville who was expecting to be there around two. According to her message, she had a couple of saddles that needed repairing. Marjorie had been coming to Nick since he started his business two years earlier. She had been his first customer. Since then, she and her husband John had sent dozens of their friends to see Nick, and he was eternally grateful to them.

Nick glanced at the clock—eleven on the nose. "Plenty of time," he said aloud as he moseyed into the kitchen for a bite to eat. After lunch, Nick walked down to the pasture to check on the horses. He took his time getting down the hill, admiring the endless blue sky above him. It was the perfect fall day, with a temperature in the low seventies and only a hint of a breeze. Days like this were the reason he had chosen East Tennessee.

As he approached the fence, a pair of horses named Shadow and Cinnamon walked over to greet him.

"Hey girls," he said as they lowered their heads and brushed against him. "How are you today?"

He talked to them for a few minutes, the way a parent would a child, then looked them over from tip to tail to ensure they were healthy. Satisfied with their condition, he grabbed a saddle from inside the stables and placed it on Shadow.

"You'll have your turn tomorrow," he told Cinnamon as she watched with envy.

Nick took off across the pasture toward the woods, on the same path as always. He'd gotten the old Caldwell Farm for a steal when it had come up for sale three years earlier. He had been searching for a place where his horses would have more room, and the fifty acres of pasture and woods were the perfect spot. His property stretched from the highway at the bottom of the hill to the top of the ridge and down the other side, ending at the water's edge. Aside from the sprawling pastures, there were ponds and creeks and paths to walk and ride. He never got bored, and neither did the horses. In his mind, a better property didn't exist anywhere on God's green earth.

As he ascended the hill, he thought once more of Eve. As he recounted their conversation, he fought to suppress a smile. But a few seconds later, Nick caught himself. Ashamed, he looked to the heavens and whispered, "I'm sorry."

When he crested the ridge, he stopped and turned back. With the trees alive and vibrant beneath the midday sun, the view of the valley below was spectacular. He considered heading back, but Shadow appeared to have other plans. Bending her head toward the lake, she beckoned Nick forward. A check of the time told him he still had over an hour before Marjorie would be there, so he took off down the slope in a full gallop, coming to a stop only when they had reached the edge of the water. Having exhausted herself from the descent, Shadow drank from the lake while he skipped rocks effortlessly across the smooth surface of the water.

After a few minutes, when both he and Shadow were fully rested, he climbed onto the saddle and pointed her back up the hill.

Before Marjorie arrived, Nick returned Shadow to the pasture and hosed her down. Then he went inside his workshop and flipped on the lights, found the radio, and turned the dial until he found a soft rock station. Grabbing the broom from the corner, he went about sweeping the floors.

At five minutes before two, he heard a vehicle approaching.

Right on time, he thought as he glanced down at his watch. He went to the window and observed a blue Chevy Silverado ascending the hill. The truck slowed, then came to a stop just feet from the workshop.

A tall and slender woman with dusty hair stepped out and stretched her legs when the dust cleared. She wore a Stetson and a pink shirt that was tucked neatly into her jeans. Around her waist was a brown leather belt with a gold belt buckle that glittered in the sunlight.

"My, my, my," she began as her crystal-blue eyes found Nick. "You get more handsome every time I see you. Must be something in the water up here."

Even at fifty-four, Marjorie Cantrell still had a reputation for being flirtatious. It was all innocent, of course, but she seemed to take great pleasure in it.

"Don't let John hear you say that," Nick joked as he went out to greet her.

"How are you, darling?" She hugged him.

"Doing well, Marjorie. It's good to see you."

"You too," she said as they separated.

"Your message sounded urgent. What do you have for me today?"

"A couple of saddles that need fixing. They belonged to the girls when they were growing up. I'm thinking of handing them down to the grandkids for their birthday, but they need some TLC. Do you think you could work your magic?"

Nick went to the truck bed to have a look. The leather was dry, rotted in several places, but nothing he couldn't fix.

"Shouldn't be any problem," he said optimistically.

"That's what I was hoping you'd say." She grinned. "I'm also in the market for a pair of riding boots. Got anything new since the last time I was here?"

"A shipment came in just this last week. Look around while I get these into the shop."

Marjorie went inside while Nick lowered the tailgate. He

stacked the saddles and carried them to the part of the barn where his workshop was located. Then, once he had them secured on the benches, he opened the door that led to the store and joined Marjorie.

"Find anything you like?" He slid the door closed behind him.

"Sure did." She held up a pair of brown leather boots. "You've doubled your inventory since I was last here. That must mean business is booming?"

"Picking up," he said modestly. "It's taken a while, but I think the word is finally getting around."

"Good for you," she said, looking at him. "I'm glad. You have an eye for this sort of thing, and your attention to detail is impeccable. I've meant to tell you John and I have some friends who own a farm in Rutledge. Dan and Marlene Bitter are their names. They'll be paying you a visit in a few weeks. It should be a large order too. They've got thirty horses at their place."

"Wow." A job like that could carry him comfortably through the winter. "I appreciate everything you and John have done for me. If not for the two of you, I don't think I would have made it."

"Think nothing of it. Besides, that's what friends are for." She rifled through a box of spurs. "You know, as much as it pains me to say it, this is a dying art, and you are definitely an artist."

Nick's ego swelled.

There was no question Marjorie was his biggest fan. By accident, she had found him in the first place, but sometimes that's how the best relationships, business or otherwise, begin. When she started coming to him regularly, he sat down with her one afternoon and told her his life story. Since that day, she hadn't gone anywhere else.

"How long do you think it will take—for the saddles?" Marjorie perused a wall of bridles and reins.

"Give me a few weeks, and I'll have them looking good as new," Nick said.

"Fantastic. Ring up these boots if you don't mind and throw in a couple of bags of feed while you're at it. We just got a new colt on the farm, and he's eating everything in sight."

"Yes, ma'am." Nick reached around behind the counter where he kept the feed. "Was the colt John's idea?"

"You know him too well," she said, with one eyebrow raised. "He's had his eyes on a colt for a long time, and we found a deal we couldn't pass up. He's a chestnut named Trotter."

"Well, I can't wait to see him." Nick rang her up.

Marjorie paid him, and he helped her load the bags into the back of her truck.

"Tell John I said hello," Nick told her as he closed the tailgate.

"Will do," she said as she started up the engine. "By the way, what's going on at the house at the bottom of the hill?"

Nick swiveled his eyes to the old farmhouse, which had been in a state of disrepair ever since the previous occupants left. "Last I heard, a couple of investors came in a few months ago and started restoring the old place. Looking to make a profit from it, I guess. They'll probably have it on the market soon."

"You'll finally have a neighbor," she said, turning back to gauge his reaction. "Perhaps a nice young lady will buy the place." She winked. Marjorie was sympathetic to Nick's situation, having lost a brother when she was a teenager, but that didn't stop her from suggesting he date again.

Nick rolled his eyes.

"Well, I'll be seeing you, Nick, and try your best to stay out of trouble, will ya?"

"I'll do my best." He watched her descend the hill, and when she was gone, he set his gaze back upon the house. *Neighbor*, he thought, chuckling.

Nick went inside and got straight to work. He wasn't one to procrastinate and enjoyed jumping headfirst into a new project. The music kept him in rhythm, and if he didn't force himself to stop, he'd stay out in the barn all night. But today was different, and his mind, which was usually sharp and focused, was a thousand miles away.

A little after five, Nick got up and stretched his legs. He was tired and closed early. His hours were flexible because he wanted the freedom to come and go as he pleased, and since he'd already spent a few hours restoring the saddles Marjorie had brought him, he was ready to throw in the towel. When he'd turned out the lights and locked up, Nick set off for the house to wash up for dinner.

That night, after the sun went down, Nick went out onto the front porch and sat in his rocker while he sipped sweet tea. He enjoyed the cool evenings that fall brought, and since there would only be a handful of nights like this before the winter cold settled in, he took advantage of it.

As he sat there, staring down the hill, he thought about what Marjorie had said earlier that afternoon. For some time, Nick had been secretly hoping for a neighbor. After the accident, he had shut himself off from the world and everyone in it, but lately he realized he needed more than himself and his horses to talk to. Despite his desire to keep everything bottled up inside, he was changing, and the thought of that terrified him.

Before he called it a night, Eve crossed his mind one last

time. Whether he was willing to admit it, she had left an impression. Closing his eyes, he recalled her perfect skin, those endless blue-green eyes, and the way she looked in that skirt. When his daydream had run its course, he stood and went inside the house as he tried once more to shake her from his mind.

CHAPTER 3

THE FLYER

Twenty miles away, Eve Gentry arrived home after a long day of work. Midterms were over, but since she had insisted her students write essays, it forced her to read each one, word for word. Fortunately, she had the entire weekend to pore through them. Rather than procrastinate, which was not in her nature, she had spent the afternoon in her office reading through the first dozen.

As she entered her apartment, she flipped on the lights and kicked off her heels. Next, she dropped the briefcase, shed her coat, then let down her hair and changed into something comfortable—sweatpants and an old University of Texas T-shirt. It was two sizes too big, but it had belonged to her father before he died, so there was sentimental value.

She flipped on the TV and found a DIY show, then went into the kitchen and poured a glass of wine. After taking the first sip, she turned up the heat a couple of degrees on the thermostat and went to the couch to curl up with a blanket.

As she took another sip of wine, she thought about the hot chocolate she'd enjoyed that morning and the man who had so generously delivered it to her.

Nick Sullivan. She repeated his name in her head. Despite her promise, he had affected her. Perhaps it was his rugged good looks or the fact that he had made a special delivery just for her. Either way, he was the only man she'd met since arriving in Tennessee that hadn't come on to her with a cheesy pickup line, so in her book, he was already head-and-shoulders above the rest.

When she'd consumed the first glass of wine, Eve went into the kitchen and warmed up a bowl of spaghetti from the night before. She wasn't one to let anything go to waste. When she was full, she poured another glass of wine, then went to the couch and lay down. But before she finished the second glass, her eyes became heavy, and she dozed off. When she woke, it was after three. Dazed and confused, she turned off the TV, stumbled into the bedroom, and then crawled beneath the covers and shut her eyes once more.

SATURDAY MORNING, Eve woke a little after seven. She wasn't typically an early riser, but sleep was difficult to come by since her next-door neighbor, Mrs. Blanton, was already awake, singing church hymns to her cats. Eve's morning routine had been the same since she arrived the previous summer. After pulling her hair into a ponytail, she made breakfast, then searched the paper for a permanent place to live. Not that there was anything wrong with her apartment, and it was only a mile from the university, but ever since she'd taken the job, she had been dreaming of a place of her own. She loved the idea of a couple of acres with a view of the mountains or lake or both, though she realized what she was searching for was a needle in a haystack.

Her job at the university paid well and considering the windfall in the wake of her divorce from David, she could afford anything she wanted. Real estate was cheap here compared to Dallas, so she could get more bang for her buck.

As she scanned the paper, she circled a couple of places that looked promising with a red pen, then phoned Sally Walker, her realtor. Sally had helped her locate the apartment she was currently living in.

Sally told Eve she was free after one, so they agreed to meet in Tazewell for lunch before beginning their search.

While she waited, Eve graded a few more of the essays. She reached into her briefcase and pulled out the stack of blue books, rifling through the ones she had already graded and setting them to one side. As she combed through what remained of the tests, she noticed a piece of paper hidden among them.

"What's this?" She took a closer look. It was an advertisement for a small farm a half hour from the university. Admittedly, she wanted to be closer, but if the views were anything like in the pictures, she'd gladly suffer through the drive. Oddly, there was no name or contact information, but she assumed the owner had made the flyer. Perhaps someone came by earlier in the day and laid it on her desk while she was down the hall talking to Professor Neely. Surely that must be it.

Anyway, she took it as an omen. She examined the flyer closely and found a pair of hand-drawn butterflies in the top right corner. *Cute,* she thought. *Definitely a woman's touch.*

A little after one, Eve put on a pair of jeans and a burnt-orange sweater, then slipped on her brown leather riding boots, grabbed the flyer from the kitchen counter, and set off to meet Sally.

The Frostee Freeze Drive-In, a weathered gray building with a high-pitched roof, sat at the corner of Youngstown Road and Broad Street. The little diner had been around since the fifties and was a throwback to a time long since passed.

Sally was already sitting at a booth when Eve joined her and ordered a cheeseburger with fries.

"First time at the Frostee Freeze?" Sally asked as she observed Eve checking out the black-and-white checkered floor.

Eve nodded as she looked around.

"My daddy used to bring me here when I was a little girl." Sally reached for a packet of Sweet'N Low.

Sally was forty-six but appeared much younger. She took care of herself. From what Eve gathered, Sally's family had been in the real estate business for decades. Like many folks in the area, Sally had attended college at Lincoln Memorial University and, after graduating two decades earlier, had jumped into the family business headfirst.

"My late-day appointment canceled," Sally said between sips of tea through a red-and-white straw. "So if you have any other properties you'd like to tour, I have the entire afternoon."

"Great." Eve reached for the flyer. She unfolded the paper and handed it to Sally. "What can you tell me about this place?"

Sally looked at it curiously. "Where did you find this?"

"Someone left it on my desk yesterday. There's no address or name on it. Do you know the place?"

"Sure do. It's a short drive from here, out near the lake. The Greers used to own it, but they sold it to an investment group. Last I heard, they planned to go in and restore the house to its former glory. I can make a call and find out more if you'd like."

"That'd be great." Excitement swelled inside Eve. "Excuse me, will you?"

While Sally stepped outside to make the call, Eve grabbed her cell and checked her messages. There was one from her older sister Mel saying she missed her and one from her younger sister Cassie in all caps. CALL ME WHEN YOU CAN.

Eve found her name in contacts and pressed the button.

"Eve, oh thank God," Cassie said in a panic.

"What's wrong?" Eve whispered as she felt her stomach tighten. The last time her sister had sent a cryptic text was the beginning of the worst day of her life.

"I'm at Hammakers doing some shopping and wanted to know what you want for your birthday."

"Cassie, are you kidding me?" Eve asked, mildly irritated. "You had me thinking something was wrong."

"Sorry. I just know how you are at returning my calls." She paused. "Your birthday is in less than a week, and I wanted to make sure my gift reached you in time."

"Anything you decide to get will be fine, Cassie. Honestly, I can't think of a thing I need, so..." Her voice trailed off as Cassie sighed on the other end of the line.

Eve's younger sister had a talent for pushing her buttons. They were only two years apart, but despite the proximity in age, they weren't close. Mel was the oldest by four years, but she and Eve had been best friends for as long as Eve could remember.

"I appreciate the thought." Eve stayed calm, eager to avoid an argument. There had been enough of that at the funeral the winter before. "A gift card or a bottle of wine will be fine. You pick," she said, wishing her sister the best.

She hung up just as Sally returned.

"I got us in." She beamed as she retook her seat. "Three o'clock today. The place isn't technically on the market yet, but I convinced them to let us have a look. You probably already know this, but the real estate market has really exploded over the past couple of years, especially near the water. I'm not trying to rush you, but if you like what you see today, it may be in your best interest to put in an offer."

Part of what Sally was saying was the truth. Eve had done her research. The other part was purely a sales tactic. She had heard the same speech two months earlier when they were looking at apartments, and although she didn't appreciate being strong-armed, Sally did it in a way that wasn't off-putting.

When lunch was over, Eve got in Sally's car, and they began their search for the perfect property. The first place they looked at was on Lone Mountain Road, near the golf course. Eve liked the area and the house, but they had built it on the side of a hill, which would be treacherous in the winter. The second place was farther south in the neighboring town of New Tazewell, a couple of miles past the DeRoyal plant. The property itself was superb—flat with a fantastic view of the valley—but the house left a lot to be desired, and even though the price was right, the last thing Eve wanted was a project.

Then the time came to go to the farm, and Eve felt the excitement building inside her. She glanced down at the flyer again and imagined herself waking to a beautiful sunrise, sitting in a rocker on the wrap-around porch with a cup of coffee while she peered out across the open pasture. Perhaps a deer or two would drink from the stream that skirted the property. A scene from a novel, or at least a Hallmark movie, took shape in her mind.

They turned off Highway 33 and onto a narrow and winding road framed by enormous, beautiful oaks. Once they passed the hairpin turn, the road straightened and broke free of the trees, revealing wave after wave of gorgeous rolling farmland.

"It's beautiful out here." Eve took in the scenery.

"Yes, it is." Sally searched for the driveway, then pointed off to the right. "There."

As the white farmhouse with black shutters came into view, Eve's eye lit up. It was precisely how she had pictured it in her mind. Sally turned on the signal light and slowed the car, allowing a pickup to exit the drive before she turned in.

"16 Valley Road," Sally announced as she came to a stop in front of the house.

Eve didn't say a word. She was too busy taking in the surroundings.

"Come on," Sally said as she exited the car.

She seemed nearly as anxious as Eve to see the inside of the house. After all, this was a fantastic property, and even if Eve didn't buy it, someone would. She was probably already calculating the commission in her head.

They found the key beneath the mat, then unlocked the door and went inside. The entire house had been refurbished down to the hardwood floors and crown molding. Most of the woodwork was original except for the new mantel over the fireplace. There were granite countertops and stainless appliances and a giant island in the center of an open kitchen with a white farmhouse sink.

"Whoever did the renovations did an excellent job," said

Sally, admiring the craftsmanship. "Looks like they spared no expense."

Eve agreed and went about the house, upstairs and down, soaking up every detail. When she returned to the living room, she peered out through the large picture windows and marveled at her surroundings.

"How much land comes with the house?" Eve tried to hold back her delight.

"Says here five acres, give or take," replied Sally. "You ready for the upkeep?"

Eve considered that for a moment. In her mind, she enjoyed the thoughts of an unkempt field with long, wispy grass, but the reality was someone would have to maintain the place.

"Surely, I can hire someone for that, right?"

"Of course."

She stared out the window again, this time setting her gaze farther up the hill. There was only one house on that side of the street, and it sat back at the foot of the ridge, a hundred yards away.

"What do you think?"

"I think I'm in love," Eve answered. "It's exactly what I've been looking for. Okay." She prepared herself for the worst. "What are they asking for this place?"

"Four twenty-five," said Sally, barely holding back a grin.

"Are you joking?" Eve could hardly believe her luck. It was a steal.

"I'd say take the evening and think about it, but—"

"At that price, what's there to think about?" Eve took another look around, already decorating in her head. "I want this place, and I'll be making an all-cash offer if that makes a difference?"

"Yes. It certainly does. Tell you what, let me make a call and get the paperwork started. I'll work my magic and call you as soon as I know something for sure. How does that sound?"

"Thanks, Sally. You're the best," said Eve, hugging her.

When they finished, Sally dropped Eve off at the restaurant to get her car. Even before she got home, Sally had called to tell her the sellers had accepted her offer. Eve's first call was to her friend Kathleen to tell her the good news.

CHAPTER 4

THE NEIGHBOR

On Monday morning, Nick returned to the coffeehouse and requested his usual. He'd spent the weekend working on Marjorie's saddles, so his hands, arms, and shoulders were all sorer than he had expected. He wasn't as young as he'd once been, and the aches and pains came with greater frequency these days.

As Joyce filled his cup with black coffee, she assumed his onetime deviation from the norm had been just that, a onetime thing, and now it would be years before he attempted anything daring as hot chocolate again.

"So how did the professor like the hot chocolate?" Joyce handed the coffee to Nick.

"Said it was the best she'd ever had," he told her with a straight face as he pressed the cup to his lips.

Joyce realized it was likely overdone. Nick always had a way of telling her what she wanted to hear, but somewhere beneath the layer of bull was a kernel of truth.

"By the way, she's nothing like I expected," he added as he reached for a doughnut.

"Oh?"

"I was picturing someone older, perhaps fifty or—"

"Careful." Joyce glared at Nick. She would be fifty-seven in a month.

"I didn't mean it like that," he chuckled, realizing his mistake. "I just meant—"

"I know what you meant," she grumbled. "So how old is she?"

"Young," he confirmed. "Thirty-three, I think."

Joyce raised an eyebrow. "Looks?"

"In spades," he said without hesitation.

The image of her in that skirt and blouse appeared in his mind once more. Now he imagined what she looked like with her hair down, gazing at him through her glasses with those mesmerizing eyes. Damn those eyes. "She's gorgeous," he admitted involuntarily as her memory played vividly in his mind.

Joyce couldn't help but smile. "Does this mean you're thinking of asking her out?" she inquired optimistically.

"What? No." He looked as though her question had offended him. "Of course not."

"Why the hell not?"

"I don't even know her," he answered defensively. "And besides, she's probably married." He didn't know if that was true, but he prayed to God she wasn't.

"Was she wearing a ring?"

He tried to recall, but he'd spent so much time staring at her eyes, among other areas, that searching for a ring had been the last thing on his mind.

"Not that I can recall."

"How long have I known you, Nick?"

"Three years, give or take." He took a bite of the doughnut and washed it down with coffee.

"And in that time, how many women have I tried to set you up with?"

Nick tried to come up with a number, but over the years, he'd lost count. "I don't know." He shrugged. "Dozens?"

"And out of all those women—and keep in mind some of them were very attractive; remember Gail Rollins? —I've never once heard you pay a compliment to any of them. Now you are telling me how attractive this new professor is. That must mean something, don't you think?"

Nick considered that for a minute, and as he did, he thought about his wife.

"That's what I get for trying to help," he said, looking irritated. "Don't worry though. I won't make that mistake again."

"Nick, you're unreasonable," Joyce said. "Do you want to know what I think?"

"Not really. But I'm sure you're going to tell me anyway, so let's have it."

"It's for your own good," she said, justifying her actions. Joyce stepped out from behind the counter and stood beside him. "I think your heart is ready to love again," she told him in a motherly voice. No one knew Nick like Joyce. She had heard his heart-wrenching story a month after he started coming to the coffee shop. Over time, they had become decent friends, and if anyone asked, she regarded Nick as the son she never had.

Nick tensed up at this. Suddenly, he felt extremely uncomfortable. "No. I can't do that to Jessica. I made a promise..."

"What kind of promise?"

Nick thought twice about telling her. "When she died, I

made a promise to her I would never love another woman the way I loved her." As soon as the words left his lips, he realized how ridiculous they sounded.

"Nick." Joyce laid a hand gently on his shoulder. "You know as well as I do that's a promise you can't keep, and even if you could, why would you want to? You're human, and you have needs, same as any of us." She smiled and sighed. "I told Fred the same thing when he and I were together," she added, thinking back. "We loved each other as much as any two people, and for a while, after I lost him, I thought I'd be alone forever. But eventually, I realized Fred would have wanted me to be happy, so I started putting myself out there again. Now, I've got Gary. He's not Fred and never will be, but that doesn't mean what we have is any less meaningful." Joyce paused as she raised her gaze to Nick's. "Listen to me when I tell you the heart is full of love, and not only for one person. God designed us to love repeatedly. That you are feeling the way you are is evidence of that. Don't deny your feelings, or you'll end up miserable. Jessica wouldn't have wanted that, would she?"

Before Nick could respond, the door opened, and in walked a group of students from the university.

He slid out of the way and stood in silence while Joyce went back behind the counter. Part of him wanted to believe her, but part of him was not yet willing to let go of his promise. He had said forever, and it would take more than a chance encounter to convince him otherwise.

A couple of weeks went by, and after all the paperwork had been signed and notarized, the old Greer farm officially belonged to Eve Gentry. When Sally handed her the keys to the house, Eve felt she had turned the page on the darkest chapter of her life. She hoped that with her old life in the rearview, what lay ahead was success, health, and happiness.

With most of her belongings in storage, Eve hired a couple of students from her freshman lit class to help her move. She also recruited her one and only friend, Kathleen Conway, to keep her company. She and Kathleen had met shortly after Eve moved to the area the previous summer. Kathleen was a beautician in Tazewell at the salon across from the bank. Kathleen had recently turned thirty, was divorced, and had a reputation for being a free spirit.

"I hate to admit," said Kathleen as she stood on the porch admiring the view, "but I'm jealous."

"Don't be," Eve told her as she appeared with two glasses of sweet tea. "Besides, you're welcome here anytime."

They sat in the rockers while the young men did most of the heavy lifting.

"I can't wait to go exploring." Eve looked toward the woods that bordered her property. "I used to spend hours in the woods when I was a little girl with my dad. He'd take us on walks, and we'd pretend the trees were talking to us." She became a bit misty-eyed. Her father had been dead nine months, and although the shock had worn off, the sting of his loss remained.

"What about the house on the hill?" Kathleen inquired as she rounded the corner. "Who lives there?"

"Not sure." Eve joined her and gazed up the hill beyond the giant oaks. "Honestly, having someone so close was the only drawback." She fretted, now regretting not asking Sally about who lived in the house.

"But what if it's a handsome cowboy who's single and lonely and has bulging biceps and a big—"

"That's far enough," Eve stopped her before she blurted out something that would make her face turn beet red. "Knowing my luck, it will be a serial killer or an old man who keeps a record of my comings and goings." She took a sip of tea.

"God, don't even joke about something like that." Kathleen visibly shivered. "What do you say we go find out?"

"Now?" Eve didn't consider herself shy, but she wasn't aggressive either. Certainly not as aggressive as Kathleen. "I think I'll give it a couple of days before I introduce myself. Thank you very much."

"Have it your way. But I'd let them come to you. That's the neighborly thing to do. And if it is a man with a big… smile"— she winked— "have him call me, will ya?"

Eve rolled her eyes as Kathleen handed her the empty glass and stepped off the porch.

"I'll be seeing you." She climbed into her black Mustang and fired up the engine.

Eve waved goodbye. When Kathleen left, she went inside and unpacked boxes. She had had the guys put them in the correct rooms, but the most challenging work still lay ahead. As the sun went down and she organized her new home, Eve's mind drifted to the conversation she and Kathleen had been having about her new neighbor.

Curious, she went to the window and set her eyes up the hill. A white truck was in the drive, and a light was on in the big red barn. Half of her wanted to walk over and introduce herself, but the other half, the cautious half, decided against it.

EVE SPENT the rest of the weekend getting her house in order, and once she had unpacked all the boxes, she took a moment to admire the work she'd done. She had transformed an empty house into a beautiful showplace in less than forty-eight hours, one even her mother and sisters would be proud of.

On Sunday evening, just before dark, she rounded up some items she no longer needed and took them down to the end of the drive. She wasn't one for garage sales, so she put out a table and slapped on a sign that read FREE, hoping that would do the trick.

IT WAS dusk when Nick returned home from the hardware store. Even before he reached the head of the drive, he spotted something strange at the edge of the road. He turned in to the gravel drive, parked, and got out to have a closer look. "Must be from the new owners," he said to himself as he pilfered through the items. Amid the pile of junk sat an old coffee table, a fan, a set of broken dishes, and some small pieces of furniture. There were also a few hats and purses and various other women's items, but nothing that gave any evidence of a man.

Just as he was about to head back to the truck, he spotted an old riding saddle sitting off to the side in the tall grass. Examining it, he found nothing wrong except for a broken strap. So he loaded it into the back of the truck and proceeded up the drive.

Ascending the hill, he slowed as he spotted a light on in the old Greer place. He wasn't much for neighbors, so he was eager to learn who had moved in next door. As he slowed to a crawl, he glimpsed a young woman through the window. She was tall and thin, and from what he gathered, she was alone. He looked for another vehicle, but there was only the silver

Accord in the driveway. *Curious,* he thought as he sped up and went the rest of the way home.

After supper, Nick retrieved the saddle from the back of his truck and took it inside the shop. After a thorough examination, he found the saddle tree to be cracked. *No wonder someone tossed it out,* he thought.

That night, Nick stayed up well past midnight, restoring the old saddle. He knew the neighborly thing to do would be baking cookies or preparing a casserole, but since he wasn't much of a cook, he stuck with what he knew. After wiping down the saddle with oil for the last time, he stepped back to admire his work. Even by his standards, he had done a bang-up job and couldn't wait to see the expression on the face of whoever had tossed it out.

The following day, he woke around six and crept down to the farmhouse. He laid the saddle across the rocker and attached a note, which he had written the night before, then returned home without being seen.

An hour later, when he walked down to feed the horses, the saddle was gone along with the note. *Must have taken it inside,* he thought as he continued to the stalls. His day went ahead as scheduled, and by lunchtime, the saddle was the furthest thing from his mind. He spent the rest of the afternoon repairing straps, conditioning leather, and working on stitching for the two saddles Marjorie had brought him.

But late in the evening, after dinner, he received a knock on the door of his workshop.

"It's open," he yelled, unable to divert his eyes.

"Are you the one responsible for fixing my saddle?" he heard a woman ask.

Something in her voice was familiar.

"I am," he said, raising his gaze to find a face he wasn't expecting to see. "You." He nearly fell off his stool.

"Nick?" She seemed surprised.

"You're the new neighbor?"

"Appears that way," she said with a bashful smile as she stuffed her hands nervously into her pockets. "Well, I can see you're busy, so—"

"No," he said, perhaps too quickly. "Please come in."

She took a nervous step forward. It had been a couple of weeks since he'd last crossed her mind but seeing him again made her blood pressure rise. "I didn't think it could be fixed. Thank you. I've had that saddle for a very long time."

"The saddle tree had a crack in it, but I had an extra in the shop, so..." His voice fell off as his gaze settled on her. If it was possible, he liked her more with her hair down.

"You must have been up all night working on it."

The truth was he *had* been up most of the night, but there was no sense in revealing that detail to her. "Nothing to it," he said modestly.

As silence descended upon them, Eve calculated the odds of him being her neighbor. *At least a million to one,* she thought.

"So how do you like the house?" He reached for a towel and wiped the oil from his hands.

"Love it." She turned her head to glimpse it through the window. "As soon as I laid eyes on it, I knew I wanted it," she added, turning her eyes back to Nick. "You own the rest of the property?"

"Everything between the trees, from the highway to the lake," he answered, gesturing with his hand.

"And the horses?"

"Mine too."

She smiled. Eve envied Nick. He seemed to have everything

a man could want—land, a job he enjoyed and had a talent for, and perhaps most important of all, freedom.

"Did you restore this one as well?" she asked, admiring the saddle that was on display at the front.

He nodded. "They're all mine," he said proudly as his eyes swept the room. "Look around if you like. I just need a minute to wash up."

While he went to the sink and scrubbed his hands, Eve perused the shop. She ran a hand against the silk blankets and rifled through the spurs. Something about it, perhaps the scent of old timber and hay, reminded her of home.

"Sorry about that," said Nick, joining her a minute later. "I've been working on that one for a couple of weeks, and I have a deadline to meet, so..."

"So this isn't just a hobby?"

"No. This is my livelihood. The bills don't pay themselves," he said, attempting humor.

She tried not to smile but couldn't help herself.

"I do most of my work in the fall before the weather turns, so I guess you could say this is my busy season."

"Well, I really love your work. You have an eye for detail, and it's obvious you're good with your hands." That last part had come out inadvertently, and as she waited for the seconds to pass, hoping he had read nothing into it, she swiped through a basket of old horseshoes.

"Thank you," he said politely. "My grandfather used to tell me the same thing—about having an eye for detail. I learned everything from him. He said I had a gift for finding the beauty in the leather and making it come to life."

The sound of his voice set her at ease. She could listen to him talk for hours, but she was careful not to let herself fall into that trap. The last time she let someone in, it ended with her walking in on him and her best friend in a compromising position. The thought of that erased what remained of her smile.

"So I take it you're into horses?"

"Was," she said glumly. "Before I broke my collarbone." She pointed to a two-inch scar between her neck and left shoulder.

"Ouch. Sorry to hear that. I've had my share of bumps and bruises along the way as well." He'd broken a leg, arm, and tailbone, all at different times and all by the age of sixteen, but he didn't see the need to turn this into a contest of wounds. "They say the best way to get over a fall is to—"

"Get back up on the horse. Yeah, I've heard that one before."

"Okay." *That* struck a nerve. "Well, if you ever want to get back into it, I've got two mares who love to be ridden."

She wasn't interested in his offer but talked about the horses anyway. "They're beautiful animals," she said as she kept her distance. "I've seen them from the house. One's a palomino, and the other…?"

"Cinnamon is my palomino," Nick confirmed. "Shadow is an American Paint. I used to have another Paint named Captain, but I lost him a while back."

Eve could tell it pained him to talk about it.

"I'm sorry," she said. "But the others are gorgeous."

"Thanks. They're like members of the family."

She wanted to ask if he had any family, but as she glanced down at his hand, it was still void of a ring, not to mention the fact that she had seen no one else on the property other than him.

"Well, I suppose I should get back," she said, looking over her shoulder as the light faded. She lingered for another moment, hoping he would ask her to stay, but when he didn't, she thanked him again, then returned home.

CHAPTER 5

DINNER FOR TWO

Eve had been in her new home for two weeks when the loneliness crept in. Living in the country vastly differed from her apartment near school. On any night, there had been parties or at least the sound of tenants coming and going, and of course there was Mrs. Blanton and her singing. The farm, on the other hand, was quiet. Perhaps too quiet. Not that she didn't enjoy the tranquility, especially at the end of a long week, but she missed having someone to talk to.

She had spent her thirty-fourth birthday in Knoxville with Kathleen and her friends, and despite enjoying herself, the group was a little too wild for her liking. So aside from her colleagues at work and Kathleen, she didn't have anyone with whom she could share her day.

Rather than spend another night watching reruns of *Grey's Anatomy*, Eve summoned the courage to walk up the hill and ask Nick if he would like to join her for dinner. They had talked a couple of times, and although he appeared guarded, which she presumed was because of his divorce, he hadn't given her the impression he wasn't interested. Besides, she believed if you wanted an answer to a question, just come out and ask.

At first, Nick said nothing when she asked if he would like to join her. Her question had undoubtedly caught him off guard. But once he'd collected his thoughts, he thanked her for the invite, then kindly declined.

"Why not?" Eve asked, recognizing that his refusal was half-hearted.

His eyes grew wide. "I… um…"

"Tell you what," she said, sensing his trepidation. "I'm going home to grill out a couple of ribeye steaks I got at the store this week, and I may even bake a potato. If you're interested, join me in about forty-five minutes."

She paused, and after seeing that he was still on the fence, leaned in and said, "Listen, I'm not down on one knee proposing here. I'm just… well, to tell you the truth, I'm lonely. I'm new here and don't really know anyone, and you seem like a decent guy I could have an adult conversation with." She paused and let out a sigh. "That's the Eve Gentry sales pitch. I know it's not great, but it's all I got."

He could tell by her expression it had taken a great deal of courage for her to admit that to him.

"Like I said, forty-five minutes, and if not, I understand." She backed off the porch.

Nick stood in the doorway and watched as she retreated down the hill. Closing the door, he breathed a sigh of relief, but somewhere deep down, he knew he was in trouble.

EVE HAD MASTERED the art of grilling by watching her father. Although he had never said it aloud, she was his favorite, and any chance he had to teach her things like grilling steaks or fixing cars, he did so with the greatest of pride, and Eve, being the dutiful daughter, was more than willing to absorb everything he told her.

She prepared two ribeye steaks and two potatoes, just in case, but in the back of her mind, she had already decided she would eat alone. With the steaks grilled to a perfect medium, she transferred them to a plate and placed aluminum foil on top to let them rest. The potatoes were already in foil, so she opened one up, made a slit down the center, and started applying healthy amounts of butter, sour cream, cheese, and bacon.

When five minutes had passed, she removed the foil from the steaks, slathered on some herb butter, then sat down to eat. As she cut the first piece of meat and speared it with the end of her fork, a knock rapped on the door.

She crossed the living room and opened the door to find Nick holding a bottle of red wine.

He had changed into a light blue polo with the sleeves rolled up, and it was apparent from the sheen in his hair, he had added some product to it. Then she caught a hint of cologne, which brought a faint smile to her face.

"Hope I'm not too late." He handed her the wine. "I read somewhere that cabernet pairs well with ribeye."

"Lovely," she said, "and you're right on time. Please come in."

"Wow. I love what you've done with the place." He surveyed the space as he made his way toward the kitchen. "You wouldn't believe the shape it was in before."

"That's what Sally was telling me. Any reason you didn't

buy it?" She turned her gaze upon him. She had been curious ever since she discovered he owned all the surrounding land.

"I thought about it," he admitted. "But the timing wasn't right." He opened the wine to let it breathe before pouring. "Anyway, I'm glad I didn't," he said without thinking.

Her eyebrows went up.

"I mean, for your sake," he replied quickly, trying his best to recover.

"Right." She fixed him a plate.

Then they sat down and enjoyed the dinner Eve had prepared. The conversation began innocently. They spoke of work and the weather, and when Nick had a couple of glasses of wine in him, he opened up about his life before moving to Tennessee.

He explained that he had grown up in a small town outside Roanoke, where his father had been a manager at an appliance store and his mother a high school math teacher. He told her about his brother, Steve, who was a year older, and about how he was a colonel in the Army. Then he explained how he had once been part of a large accounting firm outside Washington, DC. Something Eve had difficulty picturing.

"I'm sorry." She tried her best not to laugh. "But somehow the thought of you in a suit and tie, sitting behind a desk, is amusing."

Nick laughed with her. "What can I say? I'm good with numbers. I always have been, but that work wasn't for me. This life suits me much better."

"Yeah, I can see that." Her eyes softened.

"Enough about me." He was eager to change the subject. "Tell me more about you?"

"Well," she began, clearing the table. "I think I told you before I grew up in Athens, which is a couple of hours east of

Dallas. This place reminds me a lot of there," she said in a way that told him she was fond of where she had grown up. "My daddy was an engineer, and my mama stayed home and took care of my two sisters and me." She explained she had a younger sister, Cassie, who tried her best to drive her crazy, and told him about her older sister, Mel, who she adored.

"What's it like being the middle child?" Nick asked as they moved from the kitchen to the living room.

"Well, it's not like they show on TV," she explained. "None of us were starving for attention. Mama took care of things while daddy was at work, but when he was home, he was interested in everything we had going on. They say some men are born to be girl-dads, and my daddy was one of them. Both my parents made us all feel loved, but I suppose my dad and I had a special bond..." Her voice fell off as she dropped her eyes.

Despite his buzz, Nick recognized the shift in her mood. "Something happened to him, didn't it?" he asked gently.

She nodded before turning back to him. "He died earlier this year from a heart attack." She paused as she fought a wave of emotion.

"I'm sorry to hear that," he said tenderly, becoming instantly sober. "I know what that feels like. I lost both my parents to cancer six months apart. They were older when they had Steve and me, which I think was a blessing because they had developed patience by then." He paused as he reminisced. "But they were wonderful people. I just wish we had more time with them." Now Nick was the one fighting back the tears.

"Why don't we talk about something else," Eve suggested. "I'm sure you didn't come over to see who was the most miserable." She managed a smile, but it quickly faded. She stood and inched toward the kitchen. "Want another?"

"Don't mind if I do." He handed her his glass.

"Why don't you tell me about the lake?" She refilled their glasses.

"The lake is my getaway," he told her. "I guess it was my grandparents that got me hooked on the water when I was five or six. There was a lake close to their house, and when I'd go to visit them in the summer, we'd spend all day on the water. Nights too. Those were some of the best times of my life." The memories were still vivid.

Her smile was back as she returned with more wine. "We had cattle on our property growing up, so we had a couple of ponds. Daddy always kept them stocked with catfish and bass. He taught me how to fish about the same time I learned to walk."

"Well, there aren't many catfish in this lake, but there is plenty of bass and crappie. I could take you some time if you like."

Eve thought about that for a minute; then she smiled and nodded. "I'd like that," she replied politely.

Time seemed to fly as they traded stories about their childhoods. It was obvious both Eve and Nick had come from loving families. It was equally evident that they had both endured significant losses. They were similar people, even down to their wounds. Still, Nick knew nothing of her marriage to David, and Eve knew nothing of Nick's wife and daughter and the tragedy that had befallen them.

A little before midnight, Nick let out a yawn. Eve too had been fighting exhaustion for a while, but the company had been a pleasant change of pace, and she hated to see the evening end.

"I think we've had enough fun for one night," Eve announced as she cleared the empty wineglasses from the coffee table.

"You're right. It's late." Nick glanced at his watch. He stood slowly and stretched. "Are you sure you don't need any help cleaning things up? I feel bad considering I'm responsible for at least half the mess."

"I got it." She ran water over the glasses and placed them in the sink. "Besides, I won't do too much tonight. Most of this can wait until morning."

"Well, as long as you're sure," he said as he eased toward the door. "Hey." He turned around when he was out on the porch. "Thank you… for dinner… and the conversation. Believe it or not, it's been a long time since I've done anything like this."

She thought about making a joke but decided against it.

"Don't mention it." She lingered in the doorway. "Maybe next time we can have dinner at your place."

Her invitation wasn't subtle, but his guard was down for the first time in years, and he agreed. After backing off the porch, he put one foot in front of the other and made his way up the hill toward home.

CHAPTER 6

SECRETS REVEALED

Eve enjoyed her wine, but with alcohol, she was a light-weight. The next morning, she slept in, and when she brought a cup of coffee out to enjoy on the porch, she noticed Nick's truck was gone, as it was every morning.

Eve decided it would be a good day to get out and explore the property. She'd been so busy with work and the move that there hadn't been time for much else, and one of the main reasons for having her own place was to enjoy the outdoors. It was a glorious Saturday afternoon, and under a blue sky and warm sunshine, she headed out for a walk.

She spent the better part of an hour meandering through the pastures and skirting the forests that lined the property. As she hiked to the top of the ridge, she discovered a path that led off into the woods. After a few minutes of twisting and turning on the path, she found herself on the other side of the woods at the edge of a wide field. She stopped for a minute to admire the view, able now to see the lake in the distance. Scanning the area, her eyes settled on a large pond at the bottom of the hill, surrounded by giant cattails. From where she stood, she could see a small dock that jutted out into the water, and at the end of the dock sat a girl holding a fishing pole.

Eve descended the hill. "Good morning," she called out as she approached, careful not to scare the girl.

"Morning," the girl replied happily, turning to Eve.

"What are you doing out here by yourself?"

"I'm not by myself." The girl grinned. "You're here."

Eve stifled a smile. "Fair enough. I just meant…"

"My mom lets me come down here and fish when I get bored," the girl said. "Says the fresh air is good for me. Besides, she's in cleaning mode today." She rolled her eyes. "And I hate sweeping floors and doing dishes, so…"

Eve appreciated the humor and smiled this time. "I know what you mean." She well recalled her attempts to avoid chores as a child. "Are they biting today?" She turned her attention to the bobber that sat motionless on the surface of the water.

"Not yet. But patience is the key," the girl replied optimistically. "That's what my dad always told me."

She reeled in the line and cast it back out into the water. She appeared to be twelve or thirteen, though Eve couldn't be certain. While they waited to see if the new cast had done the trick, Eve searched the area. Fully expecting to see a home nearby, she was shocked to find nothing but fields and forest.

"Where did you say you lived?" Eve asked, her eyes falling back to the girl.

"I didn't, but it's just through there." She pointed toward the dark woods behind her.

"Oh. I'm on the other side," Eve explained, motioning toward the trees behind her. "Is it just you and your mom?" she asked, trying to keep the conversation moving.

"My dad isn't around anymore," she replied glumly.

Before Eve could catch herself, the words were already out of her mouth. "What happened to him?"

"Mom says he just disappeared." Her eyes fell. "But I'm not supposed to talk about that," she added quickly, looking distressed.

"Oh." Eve had the feeling she'd overstepped.

"What's your name?" the girl asked, changing the subject.

"Eve." She took a seat beside the girl on the dock.

"Eve—that's pretty." The girl flashed a smile.

"Thank you," Eve replied. "What's yours?"

Just then, the girl looked up as if something had startled her.

"That's my mom," she said in a panic as she reeled in the line. "Sorry, but if I don't get back soon, she won't let me come down here anymore. Well, it was nice meeting you. Bye."

"Bye." Eve watched the unnamed girl race across the field then disappear into the woods. *Strange*, she thought as she turned her attention back to the water. She stayed there for another minute but then, remembering she was on someone else's property, got up and retraced her steps.

When she returned home, there was still no sign of Nick. By the position of the sun, she could tell it was midafternoon. With nothing else planned, she drove to Cumberland Gap and had a look around. She remembered Nick talking about it the first day they met, and ever since then, she had meant to check it out.

Eve mounted the porch to the coffeehouse at five past four. She approached the building slowly, taking in the place's charm—the trees, creek, cornstalks stacked against the white-washed exterior of the house, and of course the porch swing, where she imagined an old couple, late in years, sitting and reminiscing on the life they'd shared.

51

When she opened the door, the aroma of coffee enveloped her.

"May I help you?" A woman looked up from behind the counter.

"Yes," Eve said. "Are you Joyce?"

"Yes, I am." The woman looked mildly confused. "And you are?"

"Eve Gentry. We've never met, but I teach—"

"Professor Gentry." Joyce sounded high-spirited as she came out from behind the counter and hugged Eve, then stepped back and held her at arm's length, looking her over. "Well, aren't you just as pretty as a picture? I was wondering when we might get the chance to meet. Nick goes on and on about you."

It surprised Eve to hear her say that. Up to that point, she hadn't been sure where she stood with Nick.

"He's a real sweetheart," said Joyce. "But enough about him. What brings you in this morning—coffee, tea, hot chocolate?"

"Espresso," Eve said, feeling sluggish after her walk.

"Coming right up." Joyce disappeared behind the counter.

"These doughnuts look amazing." Eve eyed the ones behind the glass with chocolate icing. "Do you make them yourself?"

"Every morning," Joyce said proudly as she handed Eve a double shot of espresso. "Here, try one." She took a piece of parchment paper and wrapped it around the one with the most icing. "And since it's your first time in, this one's on the house."

"Thanks," Eve said, "but I'll gladly pay."

"Nonsense. Besides, if you like it, hopefully, you'll make this place part of your daily routine. That's what everyone else does. There are tables just there." She pointed to a small room off to the side. "We also have another room in the back if you prefer more privacy, or you could sit outside and enjoy this lovely afternoon. I believe there are a few tables left."

"Yes, I think will." Eve grabbed a few napkins, her doughnut, and espresso and found a table in the sun just feet away from the creek.

While there was a break in the action, Joyce turned the reins over to Sam and joined Eve.

"Mind if I sit?" Joyce asked as she approached.

"Please," said Eve.

"How is it?" Joyce eyed the one remaining bite of the doughnut.

"Wonderful." Eve wiped a bit of icing from the corner of her mouth. "I try to treat myself once a week. Any more than that, and I'd weigh as much as a house."

Joyce smiled, but she could see Eve was modest. She couldn't have weighed over one-twenty-five on a bad day.

"This is a great place you have." Eve let her eyes drift from the creek back to the house. "It's so quiet, and the scenery…"

"Thanks. Speaking of great places, Nick tells me you bought the farmhouse down the hill from him. What a lovely spot. I've driven by a few times on my way to Knoxville."

"It's almost too good to be true," Eve replied. "I was lucky to stumble across it."

"What do you mean?"

"Someone left a flyer on my desk at work one afternoon," she said. "The property wasn't even on the market yet. As soon as I saw the place, I just had to have it, so I made an offer the next day, and the rest is history."

"Well, I'm glad it worked out for you. Honestly, I'm glad it worked out for Nick too."

"How do you mean?" Eve asked.

"Having you as a neighbor has brought out a side of him

I've never seen before. He's a bit of a troubled soul." She dropped her voice. "I'm sure you are aware of his... situation."

It sounded more like a statement than a question.

Eve had noticed for some time that Nick kept his guard up, so much so that she still hadn't found the courage to ask him about it.

"Tell me something," Eve said, her mind now working overtime. "You seem to know Nick pretty well—where does he go every morning?" She had been curious about this for weeks.

Joyce hesitated. Although Nick had never specifically told her not to tell anyone, the last thing she wanted was to upset him. "I really shouldn't," she said nervously.

"Come on," Eve said. "He's my neighbor. I'm going to find out eventually."

Joyce sighed. "I suppose you're right. It's not as if it's a secret." She took in a breath. "Every morning, rain or shine, Nick drives to Harrogate to visit his wife and daughter."

Eve's anticipation quickly turned to confusion. Nick had never mentioned a family, though if she thought about it long enough, she hadn't told Nick about her ex, either.

"At the cemetery," Joyce added.

"Cemetery? I don't understand." Eve struggled to connect the dots in her mind.

"Nick's family... they're dead," Joyce said somberly. "It happened a few years ago, just before Christmas. They were coming back from Knoxville when a drunk driver ran into them on the bridge out by the lake. Nick wasn't with them, thank God. I'll spare you the details, but their car went over the side, and they drowned."

Eve didn't know what to say. No wonder Nick was so reluctant to go anywhere or do anything. He hadn't been in the accident himself, yet in a way, he had been mortally wounded, and wounds like that took years or decades to overcome, sometimes never.

"And that's why he's so guarded, isn't it?" Eve asked in a hollow voice, feeling as though the wind had been knocked out of her.

Joyce nodded. "He started coming by the coffeehouse not long after that, and that's when I came to know him. My husband and I didn't have any children, but Nick is like a son to me. It was a year before he told me what had happened to his wife and daughter, and ever since then, I've sort of watched over him the way a mother would."

"You're a sweet person, and Nick is lucky to have someone like you in his life." Eve forced a smile.

"I could say the same about you," said Joyce. "Like I told you before... since he met you, I see something different in him, as if he's awakened from a deep sleep. There's life in him that wasn't there before." She gazed at the creek. "Promise me one thing. No matter what happens between the two of you, whether you remain friends or something more, that you won't break his heart. That man has endured more than anyone should have to. He may look tough, but his heart is fragile."

Suddenly, Eve felt an enormous weight on her shoulders. She had no intentions of hurting Nick, now or ever, but she had learned never to say never.

"I don't know what the future holds." She laid a hand on top of Joyce's. "But I promise to always treat him with respect and do my best not to hurt him."

Joyce knew that was all Eve could promise. She too knew life was unpredictable. "Then that's good enough for me. I'm afraid I need to get back." A line had formed and was halfway down the sidewalk. "It was nice meeting you, and thank you for allowing me to talk with you. I hope to see you soon."

"Yes, you too. And I'll definitely be back."

When Joyce left, Eve sat for a while and stared out at the trees as the late afternoon sunlight broke through the leaves and danced on the grass. Her thoughts were squarely on Nick, and as she imagined what it would be like to lose a spouse and a child, an icy chill washed over her.

ON THE DRIVE HOME, Eve could hardly concentrate. She was thinking about the story Joyce had told her. *Poor Nick*, she thought as she almost ran a red light, narrowly missing a car. She now knew why he kept his distance.

By the time she returned home, the sun was low in the evening sky. What had been a beautiful day ended with a magnificent sunset, the sky awash in shades of red and purple. Out of instinct, she glanced up the hill. Still no sign of Nick.

She ate dinner alone and watched television for a couple of hours before trudging up the stairs to bed. The dinner she'd had the night before had spoiled her, and she missed Nick's company. It didn't hurt that he was strikingly handsome. The promise she'd made about not getting involved with anyone was beginning to feel less than useful. As she closed her eyes and drifted off to sleep, it was impossible to keep Nick out of her thoughts.

The next morning, Eve awoke to the sound of rain hitting the roof. Storms had rolled in during the night, and the leaves, which had been brilliant and bursting with color the day before, were drab and scattered all over the yard.

After breakfast, she got dressed and turned up the heat. The wind howled, and the air was noticeably colder. Fall was ending, and soon the dark days of winter would be upon her.

Just before noon, the rain ended, and the sun broke free of the clouds. Eve was sitting in the kitchen reading when she heard vehicles approaching. She sprang from her chair and went to the window to have a look. A blue Chevy pickup was out front, followed closely by Nick's white truck.

They parked in front of Nick's workshop. Out of the blue pickup stepped a tall and slender woman, whose age was undeterminable at that distance. *Girlfriend?*

Before Eve could catch herself, a wave of jealousy overtook her. It was the same feeling she had when she and David were together. She continued to watch Nick and this mystery woman as they disappeared into the shop. Eve remained glued to the window, unable to look away. A few minutes later, they appeared once more. Nick was carrying two saddles, which he loaded into the bed of the blue pickup.

As she watched the woman get into her truck to leave, Eve's eyes were set squarely on Nick. Surely, if he had been interested in this woman, he would have at least hugged her, but he kept his distance. She felt marginally better.

When the woman drove away, Eve walked up to Nick's shop to talk to him.

"Long time no see," she said, stopping at the door.

"Eve. What a nice surprise." He looked happy to see her.

She could tell he was in a good mood.

"I saw you come up the drive, so I thought I'd say hello." She paused, during which she pieced together what she was going to say next. "That woman," she began, playing nervously with her fingers, "the one in the blue truck. Is she a customer of yours?" Subtlety wasn't her strong suit.

"My best customer." Thankfully, Nick seemed blissfully

unaware of the intent of her question. "That was Marjorie, the one I was telling you about. She and her husband run one of the largest horse farms in East Tennessee. They're responsible for getting my business off the ground."

Whew. Crisis averted.

"Listen," he continued, "I hate to rush you, but I haven't had lunch yet, and I'm starving. I don't suppose you'd want to join me, would you? My treat."

Eve didn't have to think. "Yes," she said, perhaps a little too enthusiastically. The dinner at her place had gone better than expected, and even though Nick had offered to host next time, she imagined it was his way of being polite rather than making a promise. Either way, lunch was a start.

Nick suggested Mexican, but Eve wanted Chinese, so they compromised with Italian since they couldn't agree. The Pasta House sat in the center of town, halfway up the hill between the bank and the hospital. And while there wasn't much of a view, the food was terrific. The cook, an Italian woman named Josie, was a devout Catholic, so fish was on the menu every Friday. Today was Sunday, which meant spaghetti with meat sauce, a side of garlic bread, and a house salad. Nick had eaten there twice, and he rather enjoyed the atmosphere.

"So, I talked with a friend of yours yesterday," Eve said as she waited on her glass of water.

"Really? Who?"

"Joyce, from the coffeehouse. She's such a sweet lady. She had nothing but nice things to say about you."

Nick gave a bashful smile. "Joyce is one of a kind. She reminds me a lot of my mother."

Eve considered revealing to him what Joyce had told her, but she thought better of it.

When Nick collected his thoughts, he asked Eve about

work and if the university planned to keep her on beyond the end of the year.

"I think so," she said half-heartedly. "At least, I hope so. I like it here, and I could see myself staying for a while."

Nick liked the sound of that.

They locked eyes for a moment, but Josie's husband Skip brought out the food and set it down on the table just before it got awkward. Nick ordered the special, while Eve chose the salad with prosciutto and goat cheese.

"This looks amazing," she said, surprised at how much food there was.

"Few people know about this place." Nick twirled a nest of pasta at the end of his fork. "It's kind of a hidden gem."

"Well, thanks for recommending it. My salad is delicious."

Between bites, once again, the conversation came easy. Eve talked about work and her sisters, how they had all warned her against moving away from home and how her mother, someone she hadn't always seen eye to eye with, had been the one most against her decision. But as she told Nick, she was an adult and fully capable of making it just about anywhere.

Nick admired her courage and tenacity. He could tell Eve was a strong woman, and he liked that.

"Would you like to see the world someday, or does Tennessee suit you?" Eve asked as she leaned back in her seat.

"I'm not adventurous enough to want to see the world," he told her. "Once I find a good place, I stick around for a while. Suppose some folks think that's rather boring, but once I'm comfortable, why would I want to go anywhere else?"

Eve could see the merit in that. Had it not been for her ex-husband's infidelity, she too might have spent the rest of her life in Texas. But as she had learned the hard way, life has a way of pushing you outside your comfort zone.

"What about you? Do you want to travel, or are you happy settling down somewhere?"

Eve gave his question some thought before answering. "Maybe both," she said truthfully. "I wouldn't mind seeing the country. I've never been to the Grand Canyon, and I've always wanted to go to Hawaii, but I'm happy at home too if the situation is right." Her eyes landed on his.

The last of her words caught his attention, and as he leaned back in his chair, he had the sense that something had changed between them. She liked him. He was sure of it. And if he was honest with himself, he liked her right back.

When lunch was over, Nick drove home and stopped in front of Eve's place. She asked if he was interested in a slice of the apple pie she'd made the night before. He accepted her offer, and the two of them sat on the porch and continued their conversation until late in the evening.

"I was wondering if I might show you the area." Nick said as he gazed out over the field. "It would require you to put up with me for an entire day, but there are so many places you just have to see."

"All right," she said. "I'd love a tour of the area, but it'll have to be Saturday. I promised Kathleen I would help her with something on Sunday."

"Saturday it is." Nick beamed.

THE NEXT MORNING, Eve went to work and Nick began his day as usual. He showered, checked on the horses, then drove to the cemetery. On the drive over, Nick kept things quiet, which gave him time to reflect on where his life had been before the accident, how far he'd come since then, and the possibilities of the future. Even though he'd heard folks tell him time heals all wounds, he doubted whether the gaping hole inside him would or ever could be restored.

By the time he parked the truck, the sun was up, trying to burn off what remained of the morning fog. He climbed out, bringing a vase of flowers with him as he made his way down the hill where his wife and daughter's headstones sat. He'd picked that spot because of the view of the mountains.

Laying a white carnation on each of their graves, he sat and talked to them for a while as if they were there in front of him. Most days, he updated them on how things were going at the farm, the modest success of his business, and now and then, he'd let them know about the fish he caught at the lake. That was mainly for Candice. The only trouble was the conversation was one-sided.

"You girls are all I think about." He wiped a tear from his eyes. He wasn't ashamed to cry. Not anymore. Any notions he'd once had of not shedding tears as a show of strength had been bled out of him long ago. "Not a day goes by when you're not the first thing I think of in the morning and the last thought that crosses my mind before I sleep, and I miss you more every day."

He let his eyes drift from his wife's headstone to his daughter's. He paused, during which he thought of Eve. Eventually, he'd have to break the news to them as he was growing fond of having her around.

"I, um, need to tell you about someone," he said, addressing Jessica. "Her name is Eve."

There, he'd said it. He felt marginally better to have that off his chest. "I don't know if anything will ever happen between us, but for the first time in a long time, I think there's someone who understands me the way you once did. She lost her father earlier this year, and although she tries to be strong, I can tell her heart is broken." He paused once more. "For the first time since I lost you, I feel like there's a reason to live again. Anyway, I just thought you should know."

He had said what he came to say, and he sat in silence for a few more minutes. Then he got up, told them he loved them, and said that he would see them tomorrow.

CHAPTER 7

The Pinnacle

Saturday morning Nick rose early and checked the weather. According to the local news, the forecast called for sunshine and temps in the mid-sixties. When he'd finished getting ready, he added a jacket to his flannel shirt and jeans.

As promised, he picked up Eve at nine sharp, and as he watched her lock up, he realized by the smile on her face that he wasn't the only one excited about the day.

"Morning." He reached over and pushed open the door for her.

"Morning yourself," she replied, sliding in. "What gorgeous weather we have today. Did you order this up special for me?"

"Something like that." He gave a smile as they eased down the road.

They made small talk as he drove north on the highway. When he reached the town, he turned right and headed east on Highway 25. Twenty minutes later, they reached the top of Clinch Mountain.

"You're not scared of heights, are you?" he asked as he parked the truck and cut the engine.

Eve shook her head. Heights had never bothered her.

"All right then." He grinned. "Let's go."

He took her hand and tried not to notice how good it felt. He led her to the ledge, where they had the most fantastic view of the valley and lake below.

"Wow…" Her eyes swept from left to right as she took it all in. Despite the recent storms, the colors were still vibrant and glowed beneath the strengthening sun.

"It gets better," he told her, thinking ahead to the places they would see later in the day.

"Better than this?" She looked at him. "I'm not sure that's possible."

He smiled back at her, happy to see she enjoyed the first stop.

Rather than drive straight back to town, he headed east toward Rogersville, then north as he took the scenic route into Virginia. Once they reached Jonesville, they stopped on a hill that looked over the valley toward the White Rocks. The view, once again, was spectacular.

"I can't believe you haven't seen these places," said Nick as he lowered the tailgate and took a seat.

"I suppose I've been busy." She joined him. "Honestly, I've been so focused on work and the house that I haven't had time for much else."

"That's understandable," he said, observing her as she gazed off toward the mountains. "Perhaps it's better this way." Her lack of time had worked to his advantage.

"I've been thinking," she said, eyes forward.

"About?"

"Us," she said bluntly, turning to face him.

Nick felt his pulse quicken. He could tell by the look on her face there was something she wanted to say to him.

"Would you consider us friends?" she asked.

"Yes," he answered, unsure of where this line of questioning was going.

"Good," she replied, satisfied with his answer. "I think so too."

Silence descended on them, and as he waited for her to continue, he thought about all the things she could say.

"There's something I want to tell you, but I don't know how," she said. She glanced at him, then quickly looked away.

Nick was nervous. Things had been going so well. Perhaps too well. Now it appeared she had a secret. Was she married, after all?

Just then, a cop pulled up behind them and told them they were illegally parked. Nick hadn't seen a sign, but he took the officer at his word, thanked him, and in no time, they were back on the road again. With Eve's near confession still lingering in his head, he remained quiet for the next few minutes, hoping she would continue. But when she said nothing, he began pointing out landmarks along the way.

Once they made it to Cumberland Gap, Nick pulled up to the coffeehouse to grab a bite for lunch. They were both starving, and after the morning they'd had, he wasn't ready for the day to end.

"Well, well, well. I was wondering when I'd see the two of you together." Joyce greeted them as they entered through the front door. "What are y'all up to today?"

Eve turned her eyes to Nick.

"Driving around, admiring the colors," he said. "We just came back from Clinch Mountain. I took the long way through Jonesville and showed her the White Rocks.

"Ah. The scenic route," said Joyce. "It's such a lovely drive this time of year."

"Yes, it is," he replied, his eyes drifting to Eve. "We've got one more stop to make, but we decided to stop and refuel. What's the special today?"

"Chili and hot tamales," she said, pointing to the board above the counter.

Nick glanced at Eve. When she didn't object, he said, "We'll have two specials."

Rather than sit inside on such a beautiful day, they made their way to one of the wrought iron tables near the creek.

"I don't know what it is about this place, but every time I come here, it just gets more beautiful. You should see it in January when snow is on the ground."

Eve had a hard time imagining what it would look like under a blanket of white. She had only seen snow twice in her life, and even then, it was nothing more than a dusting.

"There's something about this place that sticks," said Nick as he turned his gaze first to the creek, then up to the mountains. "It works its way into your heart when you least expect it."

"I know what you mean," she said, her eyes lingering on him. "About the place, that is."

Joyce appeared a minute later with two bowls of chili, hot tamales, and a bowl of crackers. "Y'all eat up," she said, then turned and went inside.

"You like her, don't you?" Eve asked, watching Nick as his eyes lingered on Joyce.

He nodded. "She's a special lady. Like I said before, she reminds me a lot of my mother. It's uncanny. Even their mannerisms are the same. Perhaps that's why I feel comfortable around her."

"You don't talk about your mother much," Eve noted, having heard him mention her only once. "Were you close to her?"

Any smile that had been on Nick's face vanished. "Yes. We were close," he said somberly. "I remember the day she died. Dad was already gone, and my brother was in Saudi Arabia when it happened. We knew she was sick, but no one knew how serious it was. She kept it from us on purpose—said she didn't want us to worry." He stopped and gave a little laugh. "My mother was a strong woman. Before she and my father met, she'd had a rough childhood. Her dad was a drunk and used to beat on her and her siblings. So when she was sixteen, she met my dad at a high school basketball game. He told her he was going to marry her, and she said yes. A year later, they eloped."

"Wow, that took some guts." Eve took the first bite of chili.

"Sure did. But that was Mom. She wasn't afraid to take a risk."

"And you?"

"What about me?"

"Did that risk taking get passed down from mother to son?"

Nick didn't answer right away. He was thinking. "To my brother, perhaps," he chuckled. "I suppose if I think back far enough, I had some of that in me, but..." His smile faded once more.

Eve recognized she had hit a nerve, so she backed off. "Do you think Joyce makes these tamales herself?" she asked, feeling as if the conversation had veered in an unintended direction.

"Certainly," he answered, his smile returning. "I made the mistake of asking her if something was store-bought once, and

I thought she'd never let me live that down. She takes pride in making everything herself."

A few minutes later, Joyce came back out to check on them.

"Well, I see someone liked it," she said, gazing at Eve's empty bowl. "Nick, what's wrong with you?" she asked, finding his only half-eaten.

"Not as hungry as I thought," he said, unable to eat another bite.

Nick went inside and paid the bill, leaving Joyce and Eve at the table.

"I think I upset him," Eve admitted as she gathered the bowls. "Not intentionally, of course."

"Well, he'll get over it," said Joyce. "As I said, he's sensitive about a lot of things, but give him a little time, and he'll be back to his old self. So, where are you off to next?"

"Don't know. He won't tell me."

"Well, wherever it is, I'm sure it'll be good. He knows all the best places."

Nick returned and told Joyce Sam needed her inside.

After they said their goodbyes, Nick and Eve returned to the truck and prepared for their next stop.

"Which place have you like the best so far?" he asked as he backed out of the lot.

"I like them all," she said, finding it difficult to pick just one. "But the view from Clinch Mountain was spectacular."

"Good. That's what I was hoping you'd say."

As he drove out of town, the sun was waning in the afternoon sky. Instead of heading south toward home, Nick turned north and went through the tunnel into Kentucky, exited the highway, and entered the park.

"All right." He pulled up in front of the Welcome Center. "I know this is going to sound a little weird, but you'll have to trust me on this one." He reached into the glove box and pulled out a bandanna. "Please don't think I carry a blindfold around with me all the time. There's a special place I want to show you, and I want it to be a surprise."

Eve was initially reluctant, but one look into those deep, all-consuming eyes and any trepidation disappeared.

After he gently slid the blindfold over her eyes, Nick took it slowly, winding his way up to the top of the mountain. The last thing he wanted was to scare her. When they reached the top, he parked the truck and helped her out.

"Can I look now?" she asked, concentrating on putting one foot in front of the other.

"Just a little farther." He urged her forward.

It had been years since he'd had anything to look forward to, and now, in anticipation of the look on her face when he removed the blindfold, he felt as if he would burst. He guided her slowly and gently along the path until they reached the overlook. Then he positioned her near the rail, never leaving her side. "Okay," he whispered as he carefully removed the blindfold. "You can look."

When she opened her eyes, Eve swore she had died and gone to heaven. Before her, in undulating waves of yellow and orange, were ridges and mountains, interrupted only by fields of green that stretched out as far as the eye could see. Dusk was approaching. The sunlight, or what remained of it, lay across the land like a warm blanket, painting with its last rays the highest treetops. Elsewhere, shadows stole the show as darkness devoured the land.

"Do you like it?" Nick asked, gratified to see the awe on her face.

"No," she replied, misty-eyed. "I love it." She turned to him.

"To the east is Virginia." He pointed toward the White

Rocks, where they had been earlier in the day. "Below us is Cumberland Gap, and look," he said as he swept his arm from east to west, following the highway. "That's Harrogate."

"What about the university?" she asked, trying to orient herself.

"Just there." He showed her. "Most of it is hidden behind that ridge, but if you look close, you can just make out Lincoln's statue."

"How come I didn't know about this place?" she asked. "This is the most beautiful view I've ever seen. Don't you think?"

"I can think of only one better," he whispered into her ear.

Eve turned to look at him. His comment had caught her off guard, but she didn't mind. She looked around. They were the only two on the Pinnacle. As she stared longingly into his eyes, she didn't know if Nick was ready for a moment like this—but she was.

With their eyes locked, Eve smiled softly, the effect of which drew him closer until only inches separated them. Just as they leaned in, voices on the platform behind them stole their attention. They both looked up, finding a family approaching.

Eve had wanted Nick to kiss her, even with the family watching, but for him, the moment had passed.

CHAPTER 8

D<small>INNER AND</small> D<small>RINKS</small>

"Eve? *Eve?*" The second time did the trick.

"Huh? Sorry." She came out of her daydream to find Cindy standing in her office doorway.

"What's with you today?" Cindy asked. "You seem like you're in another world."

"A lot on my mind, I guess," she said, disguising the fact that she'd been thinking about Nick. Ever since they had spent the day together touring the countryside, she couldn't get him off her mind.

"I wanted to stop by and let you know some of us are getting together at Carmichael's for dinner and drinks. You're more than welcome to join us."

Eve didn't want to go, but she had put them off twice already, and the last thing she wanted was to isolate herself from her colleagues, especially since she was the new kid on the block.

"What time?" She slapped a smile on her face.

"Six thirty. It'll be a good time. I promise. They have live music on Thursday nights," Cindy added, hoping that would seal the deal.

"Sounds fun. Count me in." Eve waited until she left before dropping the smile. The truth was she didn't enjoy crowds. David had ruined that for her. Still, she wanted to make friends, and this was the perfect opportunity to do just that.

When her last class had ended, Eve went back to her office and checked her cell. There was still another hour to kill before she'd need to leave for the restaurant.

Instead of sitting in her office, staring at the laptop, she went outside for some fresh air. There were signs about Thanksgiving on the quad, which was fast approaching, and as she made her way past the library, she ran into someone she had met the first week of school.

"Eve, so nice to see you," said Scott Harper, a professor of biology. Scott was in his early forties, had jet black hair, and was a tall and thin man. He had been engaged once but never married, though most suspected it was because he was too nice a guy.

"Professor Harper. How have you been?"

"Well. Thanks for asking. And please call me Scott."

"Okay, Scott. So, what brings you to this side of campus?"

"I have some research to do in the library," he said. "How are things? I haven't talked to you since the semester started."

"Things are going well. It took a few weeks to find the rhythm but smooth as silk now. I finally bought a house," she said, trying to divert the conversation from work.

"Congratulations. Somewhere close, I presume?"

"Sharps Chapel."

He creased his forehead. "That's a bit of a drive, isn't it?"

"Half hour, give or take," she said, though it was closer to forty-five minutes.

"Well, as long as you're happy." He seemed to be searching for a bit of courage.

Amid the awkward silence, Eve could sense a question was coming.

"Well, I need to get going," she said, trying to make her getaway.

"Hey, before you go..." He laid a hand gently on her forearm.

"Yes," she said, realizing she had lingered too long.

"I was wondering if you'd like to get coffee sometime?" He conjured a smile. But it was short-lived as he saw her drop her eyes and look away. "You know what, forget I said anything." His face turned beet red.

"Please don't be embarrassed." She tried to do damage control. "You're a nice guy, and I appreciate the offer, but I just went through a messy divorce, and the truth is, I'm not ready to date again. I hope you understand?" At least part of what she had told him was true.

"Yes, of course. I don't know what I was thinking. How insensitive of me."

"No. You had no way of knowing."

Another awkward silence descended on them.

"Well, I should go," she said, easing away. "Enjoy your research... and it was good seeing you again."

She turned and quickly descended the hill, giving him no chance to reply. Eve regretted lying to him, but Scott wasn't her type. And even if he had been, she had someone with which she enjoyed spending her time and the last thing she needed was a complication.

EVE WAS BACK in her office at ten after six. Rather than risk getting lost, she hitched a ride with Cindy.

"I'm glad you decided to join us," said Cindy as she backed her BMW out of the faculty lot. "Everyone's been dying to get to know you better."

Cindy was married, but that didn't stop her from enjoying a night out occasionally.

"Me too," Eve said, realizing that outside of Nick and Kathleen, she had no social life.

As they sped down the highway, she listened while Cindy complained about the meeting she'd had with Dean Robbins earlier that afternoon. When it came to politics, Eve made a concerted effort not to get involved. In her mind, she stuck to the philosophy of work hard and let the chips fall where they may. It was something she picked up from her father.

A few minutes later, Cindy ground the car to a halt in front of an old two-story brick colonial transformed into a restaurant. It sat on the banks of the Powell River and had a covered porch with a half dozen wooden tables that overlooked the water. Despite the cool evening, an outdoor fireplace did an admirable job of keeping those sitting outside from catching a cold.

As Eve followed Cindy through the house, she took a moment to admire the beautiful rugs and art hanging from every wall.

"Look who decided to join us," Cindy announced to the group as she and Eve exited onto the porch.

Simultaneously, they all turned their eyes upon Eve. There were seven of them, including Eve, all professors of various subjects, but mainly in English or history. They were sitting at the table beside the rail, which had the best view of the water.

As Eve pulled up a chair and sat down, her eyes automatically drifted to the slow-moving river.

"I'm delighted you could join us," said Eric Fultz, a fellow English professor who taught most senior-level classes. He was older, fifty-two to be exact, and rumor had it he was next in line for head of the department. "You always seem to be so busy. I wish I had half your energy."

Eve felt flushed as she glanced around the table, only to find everyone staring back at her.

"I told myself before I came here, I wanted to make a good first impression, so I've been giving a hundred percent. I've also been a little preoccupied, what with the new place and all," she added.

"Yes. Cindy was telling us about it a few days ago," Eric said. "How are you liking Sharps Chapel?"

"Couldn't be happier." She adjusted her voice so that those at the other end of the table could hear her. Eve had never considered herself shy. In fact, when she was younger, she had been a social butterfly, but the years and her experiences had made her more reserved, and she found herself battling a sudden and unexpected case of anxiety.

"And how do you like it here in Tennessee?" asked Jamie Newcomb, a history professor and someone who was closest in age to Eve. "Do you miss home?"

Eve had to think about that for a minute. She'd been so busy lately adjusting to her new job, then the new home, that her old home hadn't crossed her mind.

"I suppose I miss it," she answered truthfully. "But I like it here. Things move at a slower pace, and I'm okay with that. This place reminds me much of the area I grew up in." Without her realizing it, a smile had come to her face. Anytime she thought about home, she remembered the days of her childhood fondly, nights spent camping with her sisters in the backyard beneath the stars or afternoons riding around the property on her horse, when life was simple, before she'd grown up, gone to college, and met David. The mere thought of him was enough to erase the smile.

By then, those at the other end of the table had lost interest and returned to the conversation they'd been having only moments before. Even Professor Fultz, sitting directly to her left, had turned his attention to a dinner roll, which he slathered with butter.

The server appeared a moment later carrying a tray of drinks and passed them around the table. Eve downed the mojito quickly, then requested another. When the alcohol took hold and she felt her entire body relax, she leaned back in the chair and let out a sigh as Adam Essary went on about an altercation he'd had with a student the semester before.

After a wonderful dinner of steak, baked potato, and asparagus, the group parted for the evening, and Cindy returned Eve to campus to get her car.

As she opened the door to her Accord, it shocked Eve to find the alcohol still had a grip on her. She sat in her car for a few minutes, trying to convince herself she was okay to drive. But no matter how hard she tried, she couldn't silence the voice of her father in her head telling her to be responsible. Unwilling and unable to overcome his ghost, she pulled the cell from her purse and called the one person she knew she could trust.

A half hour later, she glimpsed headlights through the darkness. *Thank God*, she thought, seeing the vehicle pull up beside her.

"You okay?" Nick asked as he rolled down the window.

Even in her state of intoxication, she recognized the genuine concern in his voice.

"I may have had a little too much to drink," she confessed.

Nick was glad she called him rather than risk driving. "Let's get you in the truck," he said as he helped her out of the car.

Once she was safely inside, he got her purse, phone, and keys, locked up her car, and drove home.

By the time they made it back to the farm, it was half past eleven, and Eve had already fallen asleep. Nick found her keys and unlocked the front door, then returned to the truck and lifted her into his arms. Once inside, he ascended the stairs and found her bedroom at the end of the hall. Laying her gently on the bed, he removed her shoes and pulled the covers up around her so she wouldn't get cold during the night.

As he turned to leave, she mumbled something.

"I'm here," he whispered, turning back. "You're home now, safe and sound."

It took a couple of seconds to register, but the sound of his voice brought a faint smile to her face.

"Love you," she whispered, the words coming automatically, as though they had been together for years.

For a moment, Nick stood there, frozen to the spot. This was the alcohol talking, or at least he assumed it was. Leaning over, he kissed her gently on the forehead, then said, "Sleep tight."

He retreated to the hall, where he waited for another minute, just to make sure she was asleep. Then he made his way outside and locked the front door, taking the keys with him.

That night as he lay awake in bed, he thought about those words—*love you*. Although she hadn't been in her right mind, she must love him on some level to warrant a response like that. And if that was true, what did that mean for him?

Nick waited until around nine the following day, then returned to Eve's to check on her.

"Eve?" he called, easing open the front door.

The lights were off, so he didn't know if she was up yet.

"Are you up? I'm returning your keys," he said, giving them a jingle.

Suddenly she appeared, looking panicked. "I've been looking all over for those," she told him. "Why do you have my keys? And where's my car?"

It was apparent she had no recollection of the previous night.

"What's the last thing you remember about last night?" Nick asked, closing the door behind him.

She ran a hand through her hair as she fought confusion. "I was at dinner with some people from work... at the place by the river... Carmichael's, I think."

Nick listened while she struggled to put the pieces together.

"Cindy dropped me off at school so I could get my car, then..." Her voice faded as she raised her gaze to his. "Oh God. I didn't call you, did I?" she asked, wide-eyed.

"Yes. But don't be embarrassed. I'm glad you did, considering the state you were in. How many drinks did you have?"

"A few... maybe more," she confessed, the pounding in her head returning. "Ugh. Everything is a blur." She plopped down on the sofa.

Nick sat down on the other end of the sofa. "By the time we got here, you were already passed out, so I carried you up to your room—but that's all," he said quickly and somewhat defensively. "You were pretty out of it."

"I didn't say anything crazy, did I?" She turned her eyes to him. "I do things like that sometimes when I'm drunk."

Nick didn't know how to answer that. She had told him she loved him, but how would she react if he told her?

"No." He rubbed the back of his neck. "As I said, you were out of it. I hope you don't mind, but I locked things up and took the keys with me. I didn't feel good about leaving your door unlocked. Honestly, I didn't think you'd be up this early, or I would have brought them by sooner."

"Don't apologize, and thank you," she said, laying a hand on his knee. "That was sweet of you to come to get me. I know how long a drive that is for you, but I didn't know who else to call."

"No worries. Besides, it wasn't like I had a hot date or anything." He was going for funny, and by the faint smile that crossed her lips, his attempt at humor had worked.

"By the way, who's David?" he asked as he stood.

She looked up at him with a deer-in-the-headlights look.

"You kept saying his name last night on the way home. Is he a colleague?"

She turned away, ashamed. It was coming up on the first anniversary of their divorce. *That must be it.* She struggled to understand why David's name would ever cross her lips.

"David's my… ex," she said finally, flashing her eyes to Nick.

"Oh. I'm sorry. I didn't know."

Eve recognized the shift in his demeanor. "I'm the one who should be sorry. I don't know why I said his name. Like I said, when I get drunk, I—"

"I understand." He cut her off. "Just the alcohol talking. Well, I'm glad you're feeling better, and now that you have your keys, I should get back. Lots of things to do today."

Nick turned to leave. He forced a smile, but Eve saw straight through it. Although unintentional, she had hurt him.

"Wait." She jumped up from the sofa, perhaps a little too quickly, as her head pounded again. She needed to explain but was having difficulty finding the words. *I should never have let Cindy talk me into drinks,* she thought. "I'm sorry... for everything. I made a mess of things last night. Let me make it up to you. How about dinner?" She flashed a hopeful smile.

"Thanks," he said, letting his eyes fall, "but I've got a lot of work to do today, and—"

Eve knew he was lying, but rather than press the issue, she said okay and watched as he turned to leave.

CHAPTER 9

A Second Chance

Several weeks passed, and as the weather turned sharply colder, Eve saw little of Nick. It appeared the news of her divorce had spooked him, or perhaps he thought she had a problem with alcohol. Either way, his absence left her feeling hollow.

Then, a few days before Thanksgiving, rather than sit in the house feeling sorry for herself, Eve got bold. She knew Nick would be down to check on the horses soon, so she put on a pair of jeans sure to get his attention along with a flannel shirt and a brown leather belt. To complete the outfit, she let down her hair and added her old Stetson, which she retrieved from the top shelf of the closet.

She took a few minutes admiring herself in the mirror. She had always taken care of herself, and although she was no longer in her twenties, her figure was slender, with curves in just the right places. Once she had convinced herself she still had *it*, Eve turned out the lights and set off for the stables.

Outside, Eve found the crisp morning air exhilarating. Rain

had fallen for days, so it was nice to see the sun again, and with it the promise of a new day, full of possibilities.

Not long after Eve left the house, Nick descended the hill. As he approached the pasture where he kept the horses, he noticed someone standing at the fence, talking to Cinnamon.

When he was close enough to recognize it was Eve, he called out to her. He had heard her mention riding once, and although he did not know if she was any good, she certainly dressed the part.

"Did they try to get out again?" he asked as he checked the lock on the gate. They had worked the gate open twice, most recently the previous week.

She shook her head.

He gave her a puzzled look.

"I was hoping to give riding another shot," she said, her eyes drifting from Nick to the horses. "I've seen how gentle you are with them, and I'd like to go with you if that's all right." She turned back to him and flashed a smile.

Nick's heart jumped.

"Yes, of course," he said, thinly disguising his excitement. "I'd like that very much." He glanced down at her shoes. "But you'll need the proper shoes," he stated. "Six or seven?"

"What?"

"Your shoes size—six or seven?"

"Oh. Seven."

Nick grabbed an extra pair of riding boots from the shop and helped Eve put them on.

"There," he said proudly. "They look good on you."

He was happy this morning, which didn't go unnoticed by Eve.

"Thanks," she said, admiring the way she looked in them. "I'll gladly pay you for them."

"That won't be necessary."

"Nick, that's sweet, but…"

"Getting to spend the day with you is payment enough for me," he said as he set his gaze upon her.

His word caught her by surprise, but she dared a look into his eyes. His recent distance had confused her. Perhaps she had imagined the whole thing. She had a habit of doing that. As she thought about it more, he could have been busy with orders or a half dozen other things, none of which had anything to do with her. None of that seemed to matter now because she sensed things between them were okay again.

When Nick finished securing the saddles, he turned to Eve and said, "That should do it. Why don't you take Cinnamon? She's a little gentler than old Shadow here."

"Hey, sweetheart," Eve whispered as she gently stroked Cinnamon's coat. Any reservations she had about riding dissipated as she placed her foot in the stirrup and lifted herself onto Cinnamon's back. "Just like riding a bike," she said as her eyes fell on Nick.

He looked up at her and smiled, then mounted Shadow and off they went.

Nick took things slowly, easing Shadow across the pasture. Eve matched him stride for stride. They rode to the edge of the forest, then turned up a dirt path that wound its way to the top of the ridge. Sunlight broke through the clouds, warming the air. When they crested the hill, Nick brought Shadow to a halt.

"Some view," he said as he gazed off down the hill.

Eve set her eyes on the valley below, which was awash in golden sunlight. She spotted Nick's house first, then her own.

"Gorgeous," she said as she took it all in.

Yes, it is, he thought, his eyes glued to her. After a momentary pause, he cleared his expression and asked if she would like to ride down to the lake. "I could show you the spot where I go to think." He eased Shadow in that direction.

Eve's gaze lingered on the valley for another second before turning to Nick. "Yes." She drew in a breath of fresh air. "Let's go."

As if she could sense Eve's reluctance to go fast, Shadow led them down the hill at a leisurely pace, going no faster than a trot.

"Good girl," Nick whispered to the horse, patting her gently on the side.

When they reached the spot where the trail widened and the ground became level, Nick changed course, paralleling the shore until they reached the mouth of a long cove.

Eve's eyes were on the brilliant blue sky, then the trees ablaze with light, and finally on the blue-green water of the lake.

"The water's so clear," she observed as she watched a school of minnows swimming in tandem near the shore.

"Clearest lake around," he told her as he brought Shadow to a stop.

"I can see why you spend a lot of time down here." She pulled back on the reins.

Nick got down and went to help Eve, but she was already off the saddle.

"Didn't take you long to knock off the rust." He grabbed the reins from her.

"You're right," she said, her confidence soaring. "Thanks for taking it slow."

"My pleasure."

Nick found a nearby tree that had fallen and tied up the horses, giving them enough room to drink from the lake. Then he took Eve by the hand and led her into the woods.

"Are we still on your property?" she asked as they pressed farther into the woods.

"No, but this property belongs to a friend of mine, so there's nothing to worry about."

They walked on in silence for a few minutes as they negotiated the uneven terrain. Nick led the way, but Eve was right on his heels. When the path flattened, he turned around to find her staring up at the trees, grinning from ear to ear.

"Thinking of your dad?" he asked as if he could read her mind.

She nodded. "He loved the woods. We didn't have forests like this where I grew up, only patches of trees here and there. One of them lay between my house and my aunt's place. It couldn't have been more than a mile as the crow flies, but as a kid, it felt enormous. Instead of driving, we'd take the path through the woods to get to her house. I always thought there was something magical about that place, as if it held a secret hidden from the rest of us. I know that sounds crazy." She stopped to catch her breath.

"My brother and I used to play hide-and-seek in the woods for hours." Nick moved forward at a leisurely pace. "I spent most of my childhood in the trees. Of course, my backyard was the forest, so it wasn't as if we had a choice."

They went on a little farther until they came to a small clearing. Eve hadn't noticed, but they had been climbing. Now, as she cast her eyes to the water below, she realized they were approaching a bluff.

"I love this spot," she said, admiring the view.

"So do I." He cleared a spot for them on a giant rock that was flat as a tabletop. "Listen, I wanted to apologize." Nick's tone was serious as Eve sat down.

"For what?" she asked, joining him.

"For ignoring you the past couple of weeks."

Eve pretended not to care.

"The truth is, I've been having a hard time lately, and I needed time to sort some things out. I know neither of us talked much about our past, so when I heard you say you had been married, it made me realize we didn't know each other very well."

"Nick, you don't have to—"

"Please let me finish." He drew in a breath. "I was married once myself," he admitted, his insides churning. "Not only that, but I had a daughter as well." He gave his words time to sink in.

Eve turned to him in silence.

"They died in a car accident a few years ago," he went on as he stared out over the water. "I should have said something sooner, but there's never really a good time to bring up something like that."

Eve observed him quietly before speaking. "Nick, it's okay," she said consolingly. "And I'm sorry for your loss. I can't imagine how hard that must be for you."

Nick looked at her and forced a smile, but it quickly vanished as he swung his eyes once more to the water. "When I was a kid, my mother used to marvel at my strength. She said I was the only person she'd ever met that seemed unfazed by life. After a while, I believed her. When Jessica and Candice died, all that strength was no match for the pain I felt. They were my entire world." Nick fought back the tears, and as a result, so did Eve. "I wandered around in the darkness for a long time after that. Then I met you." He turned his gaze upon her. "I didn't believe I could feel anything for anyone ever again, but I was wrong."

"But why me?" she asked, unaware of anything special she had done to change his mind.

He shrugged. "You're different. I knew that from the moment I laid eyes on you. Then, when I discovered it was you who bought the farmhouse, I realized it was more than just a coincidence. It was fate."

Eve had never believed in fate, but after finding the perfect job, the perfect house, and what appeared to be the perfect man, she was reconsidering.

"Thank you," she whispered, "for telling me." She paused and reached for his hand. "I suppose since you told me about your situation, it's only fair I tell you about mine."

"Only if you want to," he said, offering her a way out.

"David… He was my husband," she began, suddenly aware of her vulnerability. "I didn't want to say anything, but the first anniversary of our divorce was last week. I suppose that night at Carmichael's resulted from my subconscious getting the better of me. To tell you the truth, I'm glad that milestone has passed. For a time, I didn't think I'd make it a week on my own, let alone a year." She paused, taking a breath to calm her nerves. "I met David my freshman year of college," she resumed. "He was a couple of years older, and I knew the first time I met him he was the one. I was young and naive, and he was the first person I had ever truly loved, and I was convinced he loved me back. Long story short, we moved in together right after college and got married a year later. For a while, we were happy." A smile found its way to her lips but vanished a second later as she dropped her eyes. "He worked at a law firm and did well, but the more successful he became, the more our marriage suffered. I didn't notice at first, but he started staying later at the office, working nights, then weekends, and before long, I hardly saw him at all. Then, a couple of years ago, I was out shopping with my friends. I had forgotten my wallet, so I returned home to get it. That's when I caught him and my best friend in bed together."

Nick's heart broke for her. "What did you do?" he asked after a few seconds.

"I told him I never wanted to see him again. David said he'd change and that he still loved me, but I couldn't trust him, not after that. Sure enough, a month later, he cheated again. I got a lawyer and filed for divorce the next week." Eve exhaled, feeling as if the weight of the world had been lifted from her shoulders. "Well, now you know the entire story," she said miserably, turning her eyes back to him.

"I'm sorry," he said again. They sat in silence for several minutes, neither of them knowing what to say next. Then Nick raised his gaze to the sky and chuckled.

"Look at us," he said, shaking his head. "Just a couple of wounded ducks."

Eve tried to stifle a laugh, but she couldn't. "Wounded, yes," she agreed, "but not dead." She paused as her smile faded. "You know, I made a promise to myself before I moved here that I wouldn't jump back into another relationship."

Nick dropped the smile, looking serious again.

"But that day you showed up at my office with hot chocolate... I knew my plan was destined for failure."

"It's funny." He shook his head. "After the accident, I said the same thing. Only I convinced myself I wouldn't let anyone get close again. I probably shouldn't tell you this," he continued, "but the day we met, when I was taking the elevator to your floor, I kept imagining you as someone much older. I don't know why."

"Gee, thanks," she said, rolling her eyes.

"But when I saw you..." His voice trailed off, the memory of that day still vivid in his mind. He turned to her and raised his gaze.

She did the same, and for a second, they found themselves lost in one another's gaze.

"Of course, the skirt you were wearing didn't hurt." He grinned.

"Nick." She arched her eyebrows as his words caught her off guard. "I've never heard you say anything like that before."

"Well, I've never had a reason until now." He was serious again.

Silence returned as they both stared out at the water. He thought about kissing her. But it had been so long, and the last thing he wanted was to make a catastrophe out of something as important as a first kiss. To avoid disaster, he stood and offered his hand to her. "Ready to get back?" he asked, helping her to her feet.

She nodded.

When they returned the horses to the pasture, Nick fed them and gave them water, then locked the gate and they trudged up the hill.

"I hope you enjoyed the ride." He glanced at Eve, who was suddenly quiet.

"Yes, I did," she said. "Thank you for allowing me to go."

"You're welcome, and anytime you want to join me, just let me know. It can be lonely out here sometimes when it's just the horses and me. They're great to have around when you need time to think, but not much for conversation."

His attempt at humor drew a smile from her lips.

"Well, here we are." He came to a stop in front of her house, beneath the shade of the large oak.

Eve glanced at the house, then back to Nick, who had turned his attention up the hill toward home.

Rather than let the moment pass, Eve leaned in and kissed him on the lips. Quickly, she withdrew, studying his face carefully. She wasn't sure he was ready for that, but she had been ready for weeks. When he didn't react, she instantly regretted her decision.

"I'm sorry," she said, turning away.

But before she could retreat to the safety of her house, Nick grabbed her arm and spun her around, pulling her tight to him. Without a word, he lifted her chin with his finger and pressed his lips against hers. Now she kissed him back, parting her lips, allowing her tongue to touch his. Softly, tenderly, they kissed, unwilling to part for fear the lightning that had struck between them would forever be lost.

When they finally parted, Nick opened his eyes.

"I should have kissed you that day at the Pinnacle."

"Why didn't you?"

"Afraid," he said, dropping his eyes.

"You don't have to be afraid around me. I'll protect you," she said, her eyes never leaving him.

They kissed again, this time deeper than before.

Nick was a strong man, but at that moment, as the world around them faded, he realized in Eve Gentry he had met his match.

A FEW DAYS LATER, Eve was sitting in her office when she got a knock on the door.

"It's open," she said. She raised her gaze and found Nick standing in the doorway. He had ditched the flannel for a polo and had on loafers instead of boots.

"Nick. What are you doing here?"

"I was hoping to take you to lunch," he said, looking slightly out of his element.

"Now?"

"Is this a bad time?"

She glanced involuntarily at the clock. "I have a couple of hours before my next lecture, so your timing is perfect."

"Well, all right," he said, producing a smile. "Grab your coat. It's a little chilly today."

Nick helped her into her coat, and together they walked out of Avery Hall.

"Where are we going?" she asked as they made their way onto the quad.

"Do you like Mexican?"

"I'm from Texas. What do you think?"

Nick took that as a yes.

On the other side of the tunnel lay the town of Middle-boro, Kentucky. Nick found a Mexican place right on the main road and pulled into the lot. Only a few spots remained. He wheeled the truck into one, and they went inside and found a booth by the window. Chips, salsa, and two cokes were on the table in no time, and they ate and chatted while waiting for their meal.

"This is a pleasant surprise." Eve took a sip of coke.

"Things were slow today, so I thought I'd come by and see you."

"Missing me already?" She grinned.

Nick laughed. But she was right. He had missed her. The kiss they shared had awakened a desire in him he thought was dead, but it was more than the physical that drew him to Eve.

"So how is work?" he asked, thinking of the first thing that popped into his head.

"Work is good," she replied, giving the salsa and chips a try.

"Can't wait for a break though. I get a few days off next week for Thanksgiving and then almost a month for Christmas."

"Being a professor has its perks," he noted.

"That reminds me, what are your plans for Thanksgiving? Tell me you're not planning on eating alone?"

"Well..."

"Not anymore." She shook her head. "My place, Thursday morning, and before you try to talk me out of it, I've already bought the turkey and the ham, so..."

Nick's lips curled into a smile. That was why he liked her so much. She was spontaneous and demanding and a dozen other things that pushed all the right buttons for him.

"Well, how can I say no to turkey and ham?"

Their food was out a minute later, and as they ate, Eve talked about all the cooking she was planning for next week. By the sound of things, she was expecting a small army, though Nick knew it would be just the two of them.

CHAPTER 10

An Unexpected Visitor

Eve arrived home to find the girl from the pond sitting in the rocker on her porch that evening.

"Hey there." Eve smiled brightly as she exited the car, but the girl was looking up the hill toward Nick's place. "Is everything okay?" she asked, louder this time.

"I got bored, that's all." The girl turned her attention to Eve. "You have a lovely home," she said, her voice soft and innocent.

"Thanks." Eve mounted the porch. "Do you want to come in? I'm making lasagna for dinner, and there'll be plenty for both of us."

The girl nodded as a smile broke across her face.

"Your mother won't mind, will she?"

"No. I told her about running into you at the pond that day. She said as long as I'm home by dark, she doesn't mind."

"All right then." Eve found the key and unlocked the door, letting the girl in ahead of her. She dropped her purse, briefcase, and keys on the coffee table and stuffed her cell into her back pocket as she started toward the kitchen. "I don't suppose

I could get you to help, could I?" Eve had enjoyed helping in the kitchen when she was younger.

"I'd love to." The girl grinned, then joined Eve in the kitchen.

Eve discarded her jacket, then went to the fridge and got out the cheese, meat, and tomatoes, while the girl put a pot of water on to boil.

"Do you help your mom cook at home?" Eve asked, washing her hands.

"Sometimes." The girl sighed.

Eve couldn't put her finger on it, but something about the girl was unsettling.

"So, you got a name?"

"My friends call me Andi... with an *i*," she replied.

"Andi with an *i*," Eve repeated. "I like that. Well, Andi with an *i*, how about grabbing the oregano from the pantry? It's just there." Eve pointed to the small closet in the corner.

As she set off in search of the herb, the doorbell rang.

"Excuse me," Eve said as she set off for the front door and opened it to find Nick. "Hey there."

"Oh," he said, seeing she had already started dinner. "I was going to invite you over for supper, but I see you've already started cooking, so—"

"Not sure I've ever been asked out twice in the same day, but I like the way you think." She grinned. "I appreciate the offer, but Andi and I have already started making lasagna. Why don't you join us instead? There's plenty to go around."

"Andi?" Nick asked cautiously, wondering if it was a man or woman.

"Yeah, A—" When Eve turned, the kitchen was empty, and the back door was standing open. Eve crossed the floor, stopping at the table, where a note caught her attention.

I just remembered Mom wanted me home by six—raincheck on dinner.

Thanks,

Andi

"That's strange." Eve stared out the door at the last rays of golden light dancing on the empty field. She slowly shut the back door. "I can't help but feel there's something off about her."

"Is this the same girl—the one from the pond?" Nick guessed.

Eve nodded.

Nick felt instantly better.

"Didn't you say she was a teenager?" Nick asked as he reached for a chocolate chip cookie.

"Give or take a year." Eve lingered on the note.

"Take it from someone who had a teenage daughter," he began, taking a bite of the cookie. "They're strange." He paused and cleared his expression. "I remember when Candice became a teen." He leaned against the counter. "It was like a light switch flipped. One day she was this sweet, caring little girl who thought I hung the moon." He smiled, but then looked mystified. "The next thing I knew, she was withdrawn, quiet, and thought I was the dumbest person she had ever met. I'm sure it's just a phase." Nick finished the cookie, then washed his hands so he could help with dinner.

"Maybe you're right." Eve resumed dinner preparations.

Once they had constructed the layers of noodles, meat, sauce, and cheese, and the lasagna was baked to a golden brown, Eve and Nick sat down to dinner. Despite having had lunch together, they found plenty of things to talk about. As the evening progressed, Eve wondered how she had gotten so lucky to have a guy like Nick in her life.

She didn't know it, but Nick wondered the same about her.

A little after ten, Nick rose and headed for the door. Eve wasn't ready for the evening to end, so she escorted him to his house.

"You ever get the feeling you're being watched?" she said as she peered out into the endless darkness.

"Watched?" He came to a stop.

"Not like someone," she answered quickly. "More like some... thing." She studied his face, but it was clear she had lost him. "You know, like a ghost... or something..." Her voice trailed off as a chill overtook her. "Do you believe in that sort of thing?" she asked, cutting her eyes to him.

"Me? No." He stifled a laugh. "I'm not saying it isn't possible, but..."

"Oh, so you're one of those people?"

"Those people?" He shot her a glance.

"You know, the kind that has to see it with their own eyes before they believe," she said as they resumed their stroll.

"Something like that."

Eve thought for a moment before speaking. "What about angels?" She changed her tactic.

He considered her question for a few seconds before answering.

"Sure," he said finally.

"But not ghosts?"

Nick could see he was being led into a trap. "Fair enough," he conceded. "But ghosts and angels are different, at least to me."

"In what way?"

"Angels are heavenly beings, made by God. Ghosts are troubled souls, stuck here on earth to torment the living as a way of revenge." His tone grew dark.

Eve agreed but said nothing as they reached the porch.

He turned his gaze upon her. "What's got you suddenly interested in ghosts?"

"Some of my colleagues were discussing it over dinner a few weeks ago, that's all," she said casually. "I suppose I've always had a fascination with the paranormal, but nothing more than scary movies and the occasional show on the Discovery Channel. I'm not a ghost hunter or some wacko if that's what you're thinking?" She hoped he didn't think she was crazy.

Instead, Nick seemed rather amused by it all.

"I've heard stories about the Ousley place being haunted," he offered, playing along. "It's only a short distance from here."

Eve flashed a smile.

"A short distance, huh?"

"Yep. Just the other side of that ridge." He glanced over his shoulder. "Tell you what. Maybe this weekend, if the weather is agreeable, why don't we ride out there and have a look around?"

Eve looked at him again and smiled, only this time her eyes settled on his and for a second, she forgot where she was.

"Yeah, that'd be great," she finally said, tearing her gaze away. When she could think clearly again, she said, "Wait. Don't you think the owners will frown upon us snooping around their property?"

"Doubt it." He mounted the porch. "No one has lived there in twenty years. But we'll need to be careful." He became serious.

"Because of the ghosts?" she asked, suddenly nervous.

"No." He shook his head. "The raccoons."

They looked at each other and laughed.

~

DESPITE EVE'S desire to explore the Ousley place, Mother Nature had other ideas. Instead of the beautiful weather she had been expecting after reading the weather report, it rained all weekend and into the holiday week.

By Thanksgiving though, the rain was over, and all that remained was a cloudy sky and an icy wind that brought with it the first snowflakes of the season.

Eve had been up since five preparing for dinner. By noon, she was exhausted. Thankfully, Nick arrived just in time to help.

"Do you mind checking the turkey?" she asked as she plopped down on the sofa and kicked her feet up.

Nick obliged and removed the bird from the oven. It was a perfect golden brown.

"Looks done to me," he said, showing it to Eve.

"In that case, do you mind carving?" She pointed him toward the knives and cutting board, which she kept in the drawer beside the pots and pans.

"Not at all," he said, going to work on the bird. He'd led many Thanksgiving dinners over the years, so he knew exactly what to do.

When Eve had caught her second wind, she made the gravy and set it on the table alongside the food.

"How many did you cook for?" Nick asked as he surveyed the table.

Eve laughed as she sat down and asked Nick if he would bless the food. He was a little out of practice, but he gladly fulfilled her request.

They ate for an hour, and after two plates of turkey, ham,

mashed potatoes with gravy, rolls, deviled eggs, yams, and green bean casserole, they were stuffed.

"I won't be able to move until tomorrow," Nick said as he pushed back from the table.

"Neither will I," said Eve, exhaling.

"Dinner was excellent though." He was uncertain how long it had been since he had eaten a meal like that. "You are an excellent cook."

"Thanks." She dropped her napkin on the table. "Most of what I know about cooking comes from my dad, believe it or not."

"What about your mom?"

Eve wrinkled her nose and said indifferently, "I got some things from her, I suppose. She taught me how to make those deviled eggs." Nick had already eaten a half dozen of them. She changed the subject. "Christmas will be here before you know it."

"You're right," Nick replied, though with less enthusiasm than Eve had expected.

She kept forgetting about the accident.

"Are you a tree-and-lights kind of girl?" he asked, keeping the conversation light.

"Definitely. Dad used to go all out. Mom thought he was crazy, but he loved Christmas. It was his favorite holiday. What about you? Do you have a tree and lights and—"

"Once upon a time," he said somberly, then looked away.

The pain had returned to his eyes.

"I'm sorry," she said, reaching for his hand. "I shouldn't have brought it up."

"Don't apologize." He forced a smile. "Each year it gets a little easier, and who knows? Maybe this is the year I put up a tree again." He pulled away.

Eve wanted to respond but thought better of it as she helped him clear the table.

SEVERAL WEEKS WENT BY, and while Eve enjoyed the downtime that accompanied the winter break, she debated whether going home for the holidays was the right decision. She and Nick had become close, and despite the desire to see her family, she didn't want to lose the momentum she had built up with him. As if on cue, the phone rang. It was her sister Mel.

"Eve, how are you? It's good to hear your voice."

"You too, sis. Your timing is impeccable. I was just sitting here debating whether I should come home for Christmas."

Mel chuckled. "Mom and I are having the same conversation."

"You mean she's there with you?" she asked apprehensively.

"I came over after dropping Danny off at school. It's become part of my daily routine of late."

That hurt Eve. She and her mother had never been close. Cassie was her mom's favorite, probably because she was the baby. It was the main reason Eve and Cassie didn't get along and why Eve and Mel had been so close.

"And how is Mom?" Eve asked, attempting civility.

Mel hesitated, which didn't go unnoticed.

"Mel?"

"Sorry," she whispered. "Had to get where Mom couldn't hear me." She paused again, longer this time.

"What's the matter? And don't sugarcoat things like you normally do. I'm a grown woman now," Eve demanded, sensing something was wrong.

"Mom forgets things," she confessed.

"But she's always been forgetful," replied Eve, thinking of how many times her mother had misplaced her keys or searched the house for her sunglasses, only to find them stuck in her hair.

"This is different," Mel said ominously. "We went to the doctor last week, and before you start, I didn't want to alarm you if nothing was wrong."

As usual, Mel had read Eve's mind.

"So something is wrong?"

"Yes, I'm afraid so," Mel sighed. "Eve, it's dementia."

Eve pictured the grimace on her sister's face as the words left her lips. Their grandmother had died less than a year after being diagnosed with dementia, so Eve was all too familiar with the disease. Even as a girl, she remembered what an agonizing time that had been, watching a once vibrant woman, so full of life, reduced to a shell of her former self. Now her thoughts shifted to her mother, and despite all the years of turmoil between them, her heart ached.

"What did the doctor say?" Eve asked, steadying her voice.

"They want to run more tests, but he said she may have been living with this for a couple of years, maybe longer. Depending on the results of the tests, she could have anywhere from a year to ten years left. No one knows yet."

Eve didn't speak for a long time. She was too busy trying to digest the news. After losing her father less than a year ago, the prospects of losing her mother were overwhelming.

"I'm coming home," she said at once, finding a voice.

"Eve, I didn't call to shame you into coming home. Like I said, we don't yet know the severity."

"Still, I need to be there," she said, having decided. "I was looking for a sign that would point me in the right direction. Little did I know it would slap me in the face. Give me a day or two to iron out the travel arrangements, but I'll let you know as soon as I have. Thanks for calling."

"You're welcome. Talk soon—bye."

Eve hung up the phone and sat in silence for a long time. She couldn't remember when she had felt so utterly lonely.

After processing what Mel had told her, she walked over to Nick's and asked if he had time to talk. They sat on the couch while she broke the news to him.

"Eve, I'm sorry." He put an arm around her. "Is there anything I can do?"

"Watch over the house for me while I'm gone... if it's not too much trouble?"

"Of course."

"Thanks." She wondered for the first time how Nick was planning on spending his Christmas. "Hey, I have an idea. Why don't you come with me? There is plenty of room at Mom's place, and I'm sure my sisters would love to meet you. Besides, I hate the idea of you spending Christmas alone."

Nick thought about that for a minute. "You don't think it would be awkward—me in a house full of women?"

Eve hadn't exactly thought this through, especially since the idea had only surfaced a minute before.

"It'll be fine," she assured him. "There will be a tree to decorate, lights to hang, and plenty of eggnog. My family goes all out, and everyone pitches in. Besides, my uncle Ron will be there, so you won't be the only man. I know it's a lot to ask, especially on short notice," she continued, "but it would mean a lot to me."

Nick's eyes settled on hers. He could tell she was desperate, but he wasn't ready to give in just yet. "Can I have some time to think about it?"

"Sure." She concealed her disappointment behind a half-hearted smile.

"In the meantime," he began, changing the subject, "I'd like you to accompany me to dinner with Marjorie and John. She called this afternoon. It'll be an intimate dinner, just the four of us, at their farm on Saturday night. They do something like this every year." He felt bad for asking her, especially since he hadn't accepted her invitation, at least not yet.

"Of course, I'll go," she said automatically, which made him feel even worse.

"Great. Dinner is at seven, so we'll leave shortly after six. I'll swing by and pick you up."

"It's a date," she replied.

NICK WAS uncomfortable in anything other than jeans, but as he forced himself into a pair of blue slacks, he figured he had the fortitude to suffer through one night. Besides, with Eve on his arm, he would be focused on her.

He had spoken to her earlier in the day and told her to wear something nice, which is how Marjorie had said it to him—although now that he thought about it, what did she mean by nice? As he struggled with the decision of tie or no tie, he stood in front of the bathroom mirror, contemplating shaving. He ran a hand across the stubble and tried to recall the last time his face had been smooth. Deciding against the shave, he opted for a tie and went to get dressed.

When he had dressed, Nick ditched the tie after all, slid on a pair of black loafers, and shrugged into his navy sport coat. He looked good, and he knew it. Confidently, he hopped into the truck and coasted down the hill. Eve was waiting for him when he arrived.

As she stepped off the porch, Nick first noticed her strappy black heels. Then his eyes rose to take in the rest of her. Her dress was a magnificent magenta, stopping a few inches above the knees, and had full-length sleeves made of lace. The mere sight of her nearly stopped his heart.

Once he'd composed himself, Nick got out and opened the door for her. Eve slid in and flashed a smile.

"Too much?" she asked as Nick returned to the truck.

"No. You look stunning," he said, allowing his eyes to linger on her.

"Thank you," she said happily as he put the truck in gear. "I didn't know what to wear," she admitted as they turned onto the road. "I had it narrowed down to this or the black strapless, but I figured this might be more appropriate."

Nick's mind was on the black dress now, imagining the material clinging to her every curve. And as he tried to snap back to the present, he realized there was nothing that wouldn't look good on Eve.

"Well, you chose wisely." He stole another look.

They arrived at the farm a little before seven. Nick made it a point to be early wherever he went. The large iron gate was open, so he proceeded up the drive. As they approached, Eve marveled at the way the moonlight glittered on the surface of the lake in the distance.

"You weren't kidding," she said to Nick as she swiveled her eyes toward the house. "This place is amazing."

"Wait until you see the inside."

At the top of the hill, a sprawling home made entirely of river stone appeared, and there were lights all around.

"Wow," Eve said, mouth agape. "This is their house?"

Nick laughed. "And it's just the two of them." He slowed the truck to a stop. "Marjorie is from old money, and John is a self-made millionaire many times over."

Eve suddenly felt nervous.

"But you'll never meet more down-to-earth people," Nick said, sensing her apprehension. "I've known them both for a long time."

Nick jumped out and went to the passenger's side. He opened the door and took Eve's hand, helping her out. When she stood, he looked her over, still stunned by her beauty.

"Amazing," he whispered, but loud enough where she could hear.

Eve turned and kissed him, then wiped away the lipstick from his lips. "Let's go," she said, leading him toward the door.

By the time they reached the porch, Marjorie was already welcoming them inside.

"Men with manners are becoming quite rare," said Marjorie, having seen Nick help Eve out of the truck.

"Yes, they are." Eve introduced herself to Marjorie. "You have a lovely home. Thank you so much for inviting me."

"You're most welcome," Marjorie replied. "Any friend of Nick is a friend of mine. Please come in. John is out back, wrestling with the barbecue, and there is wine on the bar in the kitchen. Red and white. Help yourself."

While Eve headed for the kitchen, Marjorie stopped Nick at the door.

"Hello, handsome." She hugged him and glanced over his shoulder. "She's a looker. Better not let that one get away."

Nick smiled.

After grabbing a glass of wine, Nick and Eve joined John out on the patio.

"Nick how are you, old friend?" said John, lowering the hood on the grill.

"Half and half," Nick replied, shaking his hand.

"And this must be Ms. Gentry we've heard so much about," he said, turning his attention to her.

"Eve," she said, cutting her eyes to Nick, whose face had reddened.

"Eve it is." John kissed her hand. "It's a pleasure, and might I say you're even lovelier than Nick described."

"A real charmer, this one," Marjorie noted, joining them. "Eve, would you mind helping me for a moment in the kitchen?"

"Not at all." Eve handed her wine to Nick.

"You weren't lying when you said she was gorgeous," said John once the women were out of earshot. "Are you sure she's not a bit out of your league?"

Nick looked over his shoulder and chuckled, but he wondered if there wasn't some truth in what John was saying.

"So Eve, what do you think of Nick?" Marjorie got straight to the point.

Eve took a few seconds to think of an adequate response. "What can I say? He's the best," she replied, glancing over her shoulder at him.

"Yes, he certainly is," Marjorie said. "It's almost as if fate has brought you to him." She reached for the charcuterie tray.

"How do you mean?" Eve asked curiously.

"Over the summer, he told me he was thinking of moving on, trying someplace new. I told him to wait. Things would get better. But he was in a dark place. Then you appear, and it's like night and day with him. I don't think I've ever seen him as happy as he is now."

"To be honest, Nick saved me," Eve admitted. "After my

divorce, I was feeling low. I was listing, unsure of where to go or what to do. If that wasn't bad enough, my father died a short time later. After a few months of living with my mom, I started applying for jobs, and it wasn't long before I got an email saying a small school in Tennessee wanted to interview me. From then on, it's been a dream. Then, when Nick showed up one morning with that cup of hot chocolate, I was smitten. But don't tell him I said so," she whispered in jest.

"It'll be our little secret," Marjorie whispered back as she handed the tray to Eve.

They met the men on the back patio just as John was plating the filets.

"Excellent timing," John noted as he offered them all a seat.

When they had filled their plates, John raised a glass. "To Nick and Eve and the start of something beautiful and ever-lasting."

"To Nick and Eve," Marjorie repeated, then they all tapped glasses.

They spent several hours talking about life, love, and horses, and although Eve had only met them, she was as much a part of the conversation as anyone.

When dinner was over, Eve and Nick said their goodbyes and got back in the truck.

"You were right," Eve said as they drove away. "They are great. John is so funny, and Marjorie, what a spitfire. I hope I'm half as energetic when I'm their age and half as in love. Did you see the way they looked at one another? Oh, to have that." She sighed and gazed out the window as the world zoomed by.

Between her talk of love and the way she looked in that dress, Nick struggled to keep his eyes on the road.

"Have you given any more thought to my invitation?" she asked, turning back to him.

"Yes," he said calmly, eyes fixed on the road ahead. "I think some time away would do me good."

Eve grinned.

When they returned to Eve's place, Nick didn't want the night to end. He had already decided he was ready to love again. Eve had come out of nowhere and knocked down the walls he had built around his heart. She was beautiful, relentless, and unwavering in her attempt to win him over. And it had worked. He came to a stop in front of her house and killed the engine.

Eve looked at him with soft eyes, realizing she didn't want the night to end either. Rather than say anything, she got out of the truck and proceeded toward the front door. Halfway to the porch, she looked back at Nick, who was still in the driver's seat. She tilted her head toward the door as if to say *follow me*.

Nick jumped out of the truck and followed her into the house, closing the door behind him. She was halfway up the stairs, unzipping the dress as she went. Nick removed his coat as he followed in her wake.

By the time he reached the top of the stairs, she was standing in the hall, with nothing on but her black underwear and heels. Nick stopped at the door and admired her body in the moonlight. He found her with his hands, and as he explored her body, committing every curve to memory, he raised his gaze to hers. Smiling softly, she took him by the hand and led him toward the bed.

CHAPTER 11

THE MORNING AFTER

When Nick opened his eyes, it was still dark. He rolled over and stared at Eve's naked body awash in the silver glow of moonlight. He was in love with her, every inch of her, but somewhere deep inside, there was a part of him that still held on to the past and wondered if *they* would forgive him for moving on. As he lay there, tracing the outline of her body with his finger, he was reminded of the first time he and Jessica made love, and somewhere between his desire for Eve and the guilt he felt for breaking his promise, a war was raging.

Slipping out of bed, Nick found his pants and T-shirt, then headed downstairs to the kitchen to start breakfast. It took him a minute, but once he'd located the pots and pans, he grabbed the eggs and turned on the burner.

As he whipped the eggs to a creamy consistency, he thought about the night before—the dinner, the way Eve looked in that dress, and out of it. *Damn*, he thought as he closed his eyes, savoring those moments. If he tried hard enough, he could still feel her, smell her, taste her. She had come alive in his arms, and he had broken free of the chains that had for so long held him captive.

Footsteps on the stairs brought him out of his daydream.

"Did I wake you?" he asked, peeking around the corner as she made her way into the living room. She had put on an oversized T-shirt that stopped midthigh.

"No." Her voice was raspy. "For me?" She peered into the kitchen through squinted eyes.

"For us," he replied as he reached for the toaster. He dropped in two pieces of bread and pressed down on the lever to get them started. "I'm not much of a chef," he admitted, turning back to her. "But I make a mean toast and eggs."

Eve walked up and put her arms around him.

"I could get used to this," she said, running her hands up the front of his chest.

"Me too." He had forgotten how much he enjoyed a woman's touch. He turned slowly and held her in his arms, then kissed her gently, tenderly. Then they separated, and he brushed the hair back from her eyes. "I had fun last night," he said with a renewed smile.

"Which part?" She arched an eyebrow as she reached for the juice.

"All of it," he said, turning his attention back to the eggs.

"So did I."

They sat down to breakfast as the sun broke the horizon. It was going to be a chilly day, but their minds weren't on the weather. They spent the entire day in bed—making love, talking, laughing. It was like a dream—a dream neither of them wanted to wake from.

A FEW DAYS PASSED, and as Eve planned the travel arrangements, the reality of the situation weighed heavily on Nick. When he had agreed to accompany Eve to Texas, he hadn't considered what being away from home meant. Visiting the cemetery, as he'd done dutifully for three years, would have to wait, and the more Nick thought about it, the more he agonized over leaving. But despite his trepidation, he was a man of his word, and he went with Eve as promised.

THEY BOARDED a plane in Knoxville around four and waited for it to take off.

"First time on a plane?" Eve asked, sensing some anxiety.

"No," he said nervously as he adjusted his seat belt. "But it's been a while. I flew a few times as a kid," he told her as he tried to make himself comfortable. "Jessica and I flew several times as well, mostly short flights."

"Same for me." She gazed out the window as they eased back from the gate. "When I was growing up, Mom and Dad couldn't afford for the five of us to fly, so we drove every-where. But when I got married, David and I flew to Mexico for our honeymoon and—" She stopped abruptly as she realized Nick had no interest in hearing the details of her honeymoon. "Sorry. Habit, I suppose."

"Don't apologize," he told her. "I think it's only natural that we talk about our spouses. I mean, we were married once. No sense in denying it."

"I suppose you're right," she said, feeling better.

As the plane taxied and took off, Nick held his breath. Once they were in the air, he exhaled. As Eve gazed out the window, observing the world from thirty-thousand feet, Nick settled in and dozed off. By the time he woke, the flight attendant was wheeling a tray down the aisle with refreshments. Nick grabbed a coke and some cookies, and Eve did the same. They sipped and snacked as they began their initial descent.

By the time they landed at DFW, Nick was ready to stretch his legs. Despite the relatively short flight, he was not someone who sat still for very long, so even two hours seemed like an eternity.

As soon as they stepped off the plane, Mel was there to greet them at the gate. She spotted Eve immediately.

"Your hair," she commented, noticing hints of auburn. "I love it."

"Thanks," replied Eve as they embraced. "Good to see you, sis."

"You too," said Mel. "This must be Nick." She turned her eyes to the strapping man shouldering Eve's carry-on bag.

"Pleasure to meet you, Mel," Nick said, shaking her hand.

Once they had been introduced, Mel asked him about the flight, to which he told her everything was smooth except for a bit of turbulence over Arkansas.

"Well, I'm sure you're eager to get your bags," she said, easing toward the escalator.

Nick sensed Mel was a no-nonsense kind of woman. Aside from her personality, physically, she didn't resemble Eve in the slightest. Mel was taller, perhaps five-eight, and fuller-figured, but she had a warm smile and even demeanor. According to Eve, Nick and Mel were the same age, though she appeared much older because of the streaks of silver that interrupted her otherwise stark black hair.

By the time they retrieved their luggage and loaded it into the back of Mel's SUV, the daylight was all but gone. Nick was nervous, not to mention hungry and tired.

"Mom will be so happy to see you," Mel said as she exited the parking garage.

"I doubt that," said Eve bitterly. "We didn't exactly leave on the best of terms."

"I think you'll find she's changed a lot since you left." Mel cast an eye in Eve's direction. "Maybe this visit will give you two a chance to patch things up."

"Maybe," said Eve skeptically as she gazed out the window.

Nick sat in the back seat and listened while Eve caught Mel up on what she'd been up to for the past six months. He enjoyed hearing her boast a little, and considering everything she had accomplished in such a short time, he felt it was warranted. It was times like this that made Nick miss his brother, who he imagined was just waking up on the other side of the world.

The drive from DFW to the Gentry farm on the east side of Athens took two hours, and when they finally came to a stop in front of a sprawling Texas rancher, Nick was exhausted. On the drive over, he'd learned that Eve's younger sister, Cassie, would not be around until the next day, which meant the evening should be free of fireworks.

Nick was the first to exit the vehicle. When Mel popped the trunk, he grabbed the bags and eased toward the front door. Mel and Eve were close behind.

Eve's mother, Nancy, was there to greet them at the door. She was a wiry woman with a round face and silver hair. Her eyes were blue-green, same as Eve's, and Nick knew right away from whom Eve had inherited her looks.

"Oh, my darling." Nancy threw her arms around Eve's neck.

Eve dared a glance at Mel, who mouthed, *Told you.*

"Let me take a gander at you," she said, brushing a strand of loose hair from her eyes as she held her at arm's length. "Being away has been good for you."

"Thanks, Mom. This is Nick Sullivan," she went on.

"My, my, my." Nancy took Nick in with her eyes. "Aren't you a handsome man?"

"Mom!" Mel and Eve said simultaneously, wide-eyed with shock.

"Well...?"

Nick blushed. "Pleased to meet you, Mrs. Gentry."

"Heavens, call me Nancy," she said, circling her arms around him. "I hope you don't mind, but we're huggers around here. Please make yourself at home." She showed them in. "There's some meatloaf and mashed potatoes in the kitchen if you're hungry."

"Thanks. We're starving," said Eve, looking at Nick.

As they sat down to a late dinner, Eve, Mel, and Nancy dominated the conversation while Nick listened and his eyes searched the room, examining the family pictures on the wall. Eve's father, Frank, was the person she cherished most in the world. Even from a photograph, Nick could tell he adored the girls.

"So, Nick," Nancy began, turning her attention to him. "Is this your first trip to the great state of Texas?"

"Yes, ma'am," he said. "And if I didn't say it before, thank you for allowing me to spend the holidays with you and your family. It means a lot."

"We're glad to have you, aren't we girls?" she asked, looking at them.

Eve and Mel both nodded in unison.

"Evy has had a bad run of luck lately, so I'm glad she's found someone who makes her happy."

"Well, you have a wonderful daughter," Nick said as he

flashed his eyes to Eve. "She's been a real blessing, and I thank God every day for bringing her into my life."

Eve raised her gaze to Nick and smiled tenderly. It was the first time she'd heard him say those words, and it nearly drew tears from her eyes.

Usually, Mel would have been the first to call BS, but as she observed Nick, she recognized the sincerity in his voice.

Later that evening when things had settled, Eve and Nick sat on the couch in the living room, warming themselves by the fire.

"Did you mean what you said at dinner... about thanking God for bringing me into your life?"

Nick stared at her for a moment, unflinching. "Yes, of course," he replied. "I realize I'm not always the best at expressing my feelings, but I meant what I said. You've awakened something in me I thought was gone forever."

Before Eve could respond, her mother appeared with some blankets and an extra pillow for Nick. "There you are," she said, handing them to him. "If you need anything else, we have a linen closet at the end of the hall."

"Thank you," he said politely.

When she walked away, Nick turned to Eve. "I think that's my cue. Sleep tight." He leaned forward and kissed her on the forehead.

That night, while everyone else slept, Eve lay in bed for a long time, thinking about her life. A year ago, her entire world was in pieces. Now she had an exciting career, her own home, and a man in her life with whom she could share her hopes and dreams.

The following day, Eve woke and looked in on Nick. He was still sleeping, so she went downstairs to make coffee. To her surprise, her mother was already in the kitchen, preparing breakfast.

"Hey, hon," said Nancy, greeting Eve with a hug.

"Morning," she said cautiously, uncertain of how to act around her mother. "Something smells delicious." They parted, and Eve found a seat at the bar.

"Eggs, bacon, and biscuits with gravy," she told her. "I didn't know what Nick might like, but I remembered how much you used to enjoy biscuits and gravy." She turned and smiled. "It's not your father's, but I think I do okay."

Before making the trip, Eve had mentally prepared herself for a moment such as this.

She knew it was unavoidable that her father would come up in conversation, or she'd see something that reminded her of him. His loss had wounded her more deeply than the divorce, but since both events occurred in relative proximity to one another, the combination had nearly done her in.

"So what's the story with you and Nick?" Nancy asked casually.

"No story," she answered timidly.

"Come now. I'm your mother. You can tell me."

"Seriously. No story," she repeated, becoming irritated.

"Oh pooh," Nancy said, gesturing with her hand. "Why would you invite him to Christmas if there wasn't at least some interest?"

Eve wanted to believe her mother had changed, and perhaps she had, but she sounded like the same woman who had for years grated on her nerves with her constant meddling.

"He was alone for Christmas," she confessed, suppressing her irritation. "And I couldn't stand the thought of him waking up Christmas morning all by himself."

"Now that I can believe." Nancy flipped the eggs. "Still, it's hard to imagine a guy like that not having someone to spend Christmas with."

Eve didn't respond right away. She was busy thinking. "He did," she said carefully.

"Oh, so he's divorced too?" Nancy guessed, connecting the dots.

Something in the way she asked made Eve's skin crawl. "Not exactly."

"Morning, ladies." Nick appeared under the arch that separated the kitchen from the dining room.

Thank God, Eve thought as she raised her gaze to him. He had saved her from a conversation she wasn't ready to have.

"Sleep well?" Nancy asked as she flipped on the oven light to check the biscuits.

"Best night's sleep I've had in years," he told her as he stretched his arms into the air. "Must be the mattress. Is it goose down?"

"Yes," she replied. "Frank, Eve's father, always said goose-down mattresses were the most comfortable." Her voice trailed off as an image of him appeared in her head.

"Well, I believe he was on to something," said Nick as he sat down at the bar beside Eve. He waited until Nancy went back to breakfast before leaning over and kissing Eve on the cheek. "Good morning to you too," he whispered, giving her a wink.

She smiled as her face turned pink.

"I hope you're hungry," said Nancy as she turned off the burner. "I have eggs, bacon, and biscuits and gravy. What's your poison?"

"A little of each," he answered happily.

"I love a man with an appetite," she said, filling a plate for him. "Eve, what about you, dear?"

"I can fix my own, thanks," she replied icily as she circled the bar. Once she had drowned a biscuit with gravy and added two strips of crispy bacon, she rejoined Nick at the bar. "Did you sleep well or was that all for show?" she asked when Nancy left the room.

"No. I slept well," he confirmed. "I woke up in the middle of the night but went right back to sleep. I feel like I'm ready to take on the world today."

"You'd better be," Eve warned as she crunched on the bacon. "Because Cassie will be here later, and if I know my sister, she'll be looking to stir up trouble."

Shortly before lunch, a blue Corolla pulled up in front of the house, and out stepped a younger, heavier version of Eve. It was her sister, Cassie. The one Eve had warned Nick about. Nick heard her high-pitched voice screaming at the two kids trailing behind her even before she reached the door.

"Oh God," Eve whispered to Nick. She could feel every muscle in her body tense at once.

The front door flung open, and in Cassie walked, still running her mouth. Nick imagined every syllable was grating on Eve's nerves like nails on a chalkboard.

"There she is," Cassie said as she found Eve with her eyes. "The prodigal daughter returns."

Something in the way she said it screamed sarcasm.

Nick was next.

"Oh my God," she said, looking at him. "Aren't you a tall drink of water?"

Eve appeared mortified.

"Pleasure to meet you," said Nick. He hoped she wasn't a hugger too.

"What's that like?" Cassie whispered to Eve, though loud enough for Nick to hear.

He blushed.

After the awkward introduction was over, Cassie went through the house, searching for Nancy while her kids played out in the yard.

"Well, that was embarrassing," said Eve, hardly able to face Nick.

"Don't worry about it," he told her. "Every family has one."

The rest of the afternoon was spent listening to Cassie go on about the latest man she was with and how he had gotten a raw deal from the police who arrested him on a technicality. Eve tried to ignore her, but Nick took in every word, amused at how different she was from Eve and Mel.

After supper, Cassie packed up her kids and drove home.

"I didn't think she would ever leave," Eve said, looking at her mother.

"Who?"

"Cassie," said Eve.

"Cassie? Was she here?"

Eve and Nick glanced at one another. Before that moment, Eve had begun to wonder whether Mel was exaggerating when it came to the severity of her mother's condition. Now the reality came crashing in on her, and Eve felt suddenly hollow.

"Would you like something to drink?" she offered her mother as she rose and went into the kitchen.

"A glass of tea will be fine, dear," Nancy replied.

Eve titled her head toward the kitchen, signaling Nick to join her.

She was leaning against the counter when he reached the kitchen, her head buried in her hands. Without speaking, Nick went to her and held her in his arms. "Everything is going to be okay."

"No. I don't think it is." She realized for the first time the true nature of her mother's illness. "Mel says she may only have six months," said Eve, divulging that detail to Nick for the first time.

"But she seems so full of life," he replied, casting an eye back to the living room, where Nancy was flipping through the channels on the TV.

"The same thing happened to my grandmother when I was a little girl," Eve told him. "She was perfectly healthy one day, and two months later, she was gone. Nick," she continued, lifting her eyes to him. "I don't know if I'm strong enough to go through this again."

Sometimes Eve forgot who she was talking to.

"Yes, you are," he said with a steady voice. "But if things get hard, and if you need a soft place to fall, I'll be here."

She stared into his eyes, and she had no doubt he was telling the truth.

"Where's that tea?" they heard Nancy say, which caused them both to laugh.

CHAPTER 12

A Time for Healing

The next morning, Mel dropped by and asked Nick if he would like to accompany her to the store. She needed help carrying some of the heavier items, and since her husband was at work, she could use an extra set of hands. Nick obliged, leaving Eve to fend for herself against her mother and Cassie, who had returned.

"I'm glad you came home for Christmas." Nancy turned down the volume on the TV. "I've missed having you around."

Eve wondered if she was sincere.

"My recent health issues have caused me to stop and think."

"About?"

"You... me... us, really," she said, glancing in her direction.

Eve's eyes settled on her mother's face, and it was then, for the first time, that she noticed the dark circles under her eyes. Somewhere in the six months since she had been away, her mother had aged ten years. Between Frank's death, Eve's divorce, and Cassie's endless drama, it was a wonder Nancy hadn't lost her mind already.

"I know we haven't always gotten along." She reached for Eve's hand. "Your father was always your favorite. I know that." She forced a painful smile as she squeezed her hand gently.

"Mom, I—"

"It's all right," she insisted. "I'm glad the two of you got along as well as you did, and God knows your father cherished you. Sometimes, for whatever reason, some personalities just line up better than others."

"Mom, I always loved you too," Eve interjected, feeling suddenly small. "It's just… Daddy always seemed to understand me. He and I clicked. You and I, well, we were more like—"

"Oil and water?"

"Something like that," she said with a crooked smile.

The sound of the refrigerator door opening caught Eve's attention.

"It's just Cassie," said Nancy. "Don't pay her any attention. She's looking for the rest of the pie."

Eve's eyes tightened reflexively at the mention of the name.

Nancy frowned. "I wish the two of you could patch up your differences. The last thing a mother wants is for her children to be at odds with one another."

"One step at a time, Mom." Eve cast a glance in Cassie's direction while considering her next question. "Do you want to talk about the health issues you've been having?" she asked delicately.

"Not really," Nancy said dismissively. "Besides, I'm sure it's nothing."

But Eve knew better, and she recognized the genuine fear in her mother's eyes.

"Mom, it's okay to be scared. Besides, I'm not a little girl anymore, and I want to be informed."

Nancy glanced at Eve. She could tell by the determination in her eyes that there was no avoiding the subject. "You've changed," Nancy said, keeping her eyes glued to Eve's. "Whatever hesitation you had before is gone now." Nancy forced a smile and patted Eve on the knee. "You've grown into a fine woman."

"Thank you, but you're deflecting," Eve replied, unwilling to let it go.

Nancy chuckled. "You're right." She paused and took in a breath. "It's a little more serious than I'd like to admit. I don't know what happened. You know me, always sharp as a tack, but ever since your father died, I've been having difficulty remembering things. Keys. Glasses. Where I put that darn remote. Then a few weeks ago, I left the house to go to the store and the next thing I know I'm entering the Tyler city limits. The girls had to come get me and bring me home. Oh, it was quite embarrassing."

"Mom!"

"I know," Nancy said reflexively. "I thought it was just the stress of everything that's gone on lately, but I had some tests run and…" Her voice trailed off as she dropped her eyes.

Eve found her hand and held it. "It doesn't mean you're—" Eve couldn't bring herself to say it.

"Dying? But I'm afraid it does," Nancy conceded as she turned back to Eve. "If you'll remember, your grandmother had the same thing. The doctors say it's hereditary. So much for good genes," she said, trying to find the humor.

Eve let go of her hand and went to the window. "I feel terrible for being so far away," she said as she stared out across the open prairie. "If I'd known, I would have never—"

"Come now." Nancy cut her short. "You had no way of knowing I was sick. Hell, even I didn't know. Besides, what would you have done, continued to live here and take care of an old woman while life passed you by?" She rose and joined her daughter at the window. "Look out there and tell me what you see."

"A field," Eve replied, stating the obvious.

"That field is like life—wild, sweeping, and full of possibility. You have done something I could have never done. You picked up and moved a thousand miles away, started a new career, bought a home on your own, with no one's help. The only person I ever knew who was brave enough to do something like that was your father. He would be really proud of what you've accomplished."

Eve turned around and found her mother with tears in her eyes.

"You really think so?" she asked, fighting tears of her own.

"I know so," Nancy told her. "And on top if it all, you've got a wonderful, God-fearing man who obviously adores you. Life should be lived, not shied away from. One day many years from now, you'll wake up and realize the best of your days are behind you. When you do, I want you to look back and have no regrets. Let that be my advice to you."

Eve wiped the tears from her face, then hugged her mother for the first time in years. She was astonished at how quickly the years of strife between them had been erased in a single afternoon.

MEL AND NICK returned in time for lunch. Once everyone had filled their stomachs, Mel grabbed Eve, and off they went for more shopping. This time Nick was left behind, which suited him since he'd spent hours that morning chasing Mel all over town in search of last-minute Christmas gifts.

"Just the man I was looking for," Nancy said as Nick appeared in the garage. "I was hoping you could help an old woman and get the lights down."

"And where would I find this old woman?"

She looked at him and smiled.

Nick was tall enough not to need the ladder, so he folded it and placed it in the corner. "Where would you like them?" he asked, coming down with the lights in one hand and garland in the other.

"Porch is fine," she said. "I'll use that garland to wrap the columns. Frank always made it look so easy." She fell silent and looked away.

Nick knew what she was going through. The first Christmas, the first birthday, the first everything was the most difficult. It had nearly killed him.

Once they had detangled all the lights, they went about stringing them along the windows, the edge of the roof, and around the columns. Nick added several more strands to the bushes and the railing on the porch.

"Perfect," Nancy remarked when he was done, taking a step back to admire everything from the yard. "You've done this before, haven't you?"

"Once or twice," he said, thinking back. When he had collected his thoughts, he joined Nancy in the yard to look for himself.

"They never leave your thoughts, do they?" Nancy asked thoughtfully. Eve had broken the news of Nick's situation to her earlier that afternoon.

"No, they don't," he replied, dropping his eyes.

"Everyone keeps telling me it gets easier with time, but…"

"Easier, yes, but never easy," he commented. "Sometimes when I'm working, I get so focused on what I'm doing that I forget they're gone, or I'll imagine it's all just a bad dream. Then I'll catch myself, and it all comes flooding back. But each day is an opportunity to heal… at least that's what my doctor tells me." He stopped and flashed a crooked smile.

"I know what you mean," she sighed. "You know, Frank and I were together for forty-two years? God blessed us with these healthy girls, three grandchildren, and what I can only describe as a wonderful life. Sure, we had our moments. Who doesn't? But there isn't a single thing I'd change."

"Well, I envy you," said Nick. "Jessica, and I were married for fifteen years."

"You were young when you married," she said, doing the math in her head.

Nick nodded in agreement. "But I knew the first time I saw her I was going to marry her. I guess it's true what they say about love at first sight."

"Oh yes," she confirmed. "Frank and I were the same way. Only it was me who knew when I saw him instead of the other way around. He was an engineer. Not sure if Eve told you that or not. We met when he got out of the service. God, I still remember how handsome he was in that uniform." A shiver climbed Nancy's spine as the image of her husband was still vivid in her mind. "Eve's a wonderful girl," she said, switching gears. "And I'm not saying so just because I'm her mother. I'm sure she's told you about us not always seeing eye to eye, but she's turned out to be quite a strong woman. I just want her to be happy." She paused. "I thought she'd found that with David, but…"

"I think things happen for a reason," Nick said philosophically. "I'm not smart enough to know why, but I believe they do. Despite what happened with David, it opened doors for her that would not have been opened otherwise. Now she has a promising career and a beautiful home, and—"

"And she has you," Nancy said, finishing his sentence.

Before Nick could respond, headlights on the road caught their attention.

"Looks like the girls are back," said Nancy, sliding toward the drive. "Thank you for the help and the conversation. I think you're a decent man, Nick Sullivan, and I believe you're right about things happening for a reason. I don't understand it sometimes, but I think God did right by bringing you and Eve together."

As Mel's SUV came to a stop in front of the house, Nancy went out to greet them, leaving Nick with his thoughts.

"I see she wrangled you into putting up the lights. They look great," Eve commented as she got out of the car.

"He's a natural," said Nancy. "Once we get the candles in the windows and the tree decorated, we'll be ready for Christmas. Speaking of candles, I just remembered there's a box of them in the bedroom closet. Let me get it before I forget," she said with a wink.

"Do you need any help?" Nick asked as she made for the front door.

"No. I think Mel and I can handle it. You two stay out here and admire the lights. I'll put on some hot chocolate soon." She smiled and winked at Nick as she yelled for Mel.

When Nancy and Mel had gone inside, Eve asked Nick if her mother had been bombarding him with questions, remembering how she had interrogated every guy that had ever been to the house.

"No," Nick laughed. "Nothing like that." He cleared the

porch swing of the garland so they both could sit. "Your mom is a nice lady," he said. "I know you've had your issues, but—"

"Funny you should mention that," said Eve with a faint smile. "She and I talked this afternoon while you and Mel were shopping." She wrapped herself with the blanket. "Believe it or not, I think things are going to be okay between us now."

Nick smiled as he draped his arm over her shoulder and pulled her close to him.

BY THE TIME Christmas morning arrived, Nick had put up all the lights, cut down the tree, and hung the wreaths. Nancy had also persuaded him into fixing the leaky faucet in the bathroom, which was more his speed. Nancy enjoyed having a man around the house again, and Nick relished the opportunity to show off his handyman skills, something Eve found irresistible.

After a big breakfast, the entire family sat in the living room and exchanged gifts. There were even a couple of presents for Nick—a red-and-black flannel from Nancy and a set of tools from Eve. He loved them. As he watched Eve's family open presents, it made him think of his wife and daughter and their last Christmas together. He remembered the shock on Jessica's face when she opened the little black box that contained the diamond earrings and how Candice beamed at the sight of her new bike, which he'd kept hidden in the shed for weeks. As he reminisced, it was almost as if they were there with him.

"You okay?" Eve whispered, noticing him with a distant stare.

He nodded.

"You seem miles away."

"I was," he told her as he descended from his daydream.

When the chaos of Christmas morning had died down and everyone went to their respective homes, Nick and Eve found themselves alone. Nancy had retired to her bedroom for a nap, so they had the house all to themselves.

"This was nice," he said as they sipped tea in front of the fire. "I don't know why I was so reluctant to come with you."

"Have you really enjoyed yourself?" she asked. "They haven't been too much, have they?"

Nick shook his head.

"I've enjoyed my time here too," Eve said. "It almost makes me not want to go back."

Something in the way she said it told Nick her heart was still in Texas, and as he held her close to him, he wondered if a piece, or perhaps all of it, always would be.

Two days after Christmas, Eve and Nick said their goodbyes and boarded a plane for Tennessee. They were sad to leave but eager to get back home, back to their lives, and pick up where they left off.

If there was any doubt whether they loved each other before the trip, there was no doubt now. Nick had seen Eve in her element, around the people she held dear, and she shone like a diamond. And Eve had taken Nick a thousand miles outside his comfort zone, but he'd been both charming and engaging. The love they had for one another was strengthening by the day.

When the plane landed and they drove back to the farm, it was late, so Nick waited until morning to unpack. Eve asked if he wanted to stay at her place, but he had an early start, so he went to his house instead. As he lay in bed, recalling all that had happened on the trip, a smile found its way to his face. He was more in love with Eve than ever, but something in the back of his mind told him to be careful, that trying times were ahead. As he turned over and went to sleep, he tried to push the negative thoughts out of his mind.

CHAPTER 13

ANDI WITH AN *I*

When school resumed, it took Eve a few days to get back into the rhythm of work. Although it had only been a month, Eve had grown accustomed to waking up to breakfast in bed, or Nick in bed, or both, and somewhere between Thanksgiving and the start of the new year, she had fallen head over heels in love with him.

Now, as she sat in her office, staring out the window as the snow accumulated on the ground below, she wondered if Nick felt the same way about her. But before she could give it another thought, a familiar voice drew her from her daydream.

"Morning Eve." Cindy, sounding high-spirited, appeared in the doorway with two coffees.

"That's not hot chocolate, is it?" Eve wondered aloud.

"No," said Cindy, dropping the smile. "Coffee. Just the way you like it—two creams and a teaspoon of sugar."

It wasn't hot chocolate with Nick, but it would have to do.

"Thanks," she said, taking the coffee. "Some weather, huh?" Eve turned her attention back to the half-dollar-sized flakes that drifted harmlessly past her window. "Do you think it will stick to the roads?"

Eve had only driven on snowy roads once, and that was during a freak snowstorm that hit Dallas when she was seventeen. She remembered slipping and sliding in her dad's old Jeep.

"Maybe." Cindy cast an eye to the window. "But they say it'll be gone by afternoon. You shouldn't have any trouble getting home if that's what you mean." She paused. "So how was your break?"

"Amazing," Eve beamed. "What about yours?"

"Not as good as yours it sounds like," she said sarcastically as she pulled up a chair. "Okay, let's have it."

Eve and Cindy had become decent friends since the start of school. Cindy already knew about Nick, but only because Eve had mentioned his name once in passing.

"Well," she began, leaning in. "I went home for Christmas to see my family. I hadn't been back since I moved here."

"And they're in Texas, right?"

Eve nodded.

"And?" Cindy prodded, hoping there was more to the story.

"And Nick tagged along," Eve boasted. She let that sink in.

Cindy's eyes went up, and she grinned. "Now we're getting somewhere. Nick Sullivan." She leaned back and let her eyes drift to the ceiling. "God, I'm glad somebody finally cracked that code."

"What do you mean?" Eve asked, feeling her smile fade.

"It's just… ever since, well, you know, the whole thing with the car accident, Nick has been the most eligible bachelor in the whole county. He's been on the radar of every woman from Middleboro to Morristown, and until you came along, he was

locked up tighter than Fort Knox. Tell me, what did you say...
or do to get him to open up?"

"Cindy Bunch," said Eve, looking shocked.

"Well, there are certain advantages to looking the way you
do," she said, taking a sip of coffee.

"Thanks, I think," Eve replied, unsure if that was intended
as a compliment. "But really, I didn't do anything special." Eve
considered exactly how she had been the one to break him out
of his shell. "I guess the timing was just right." She sipped again
on her coffee. "And I may have worn those tight jeans a time or
two," she added with a wry smile.

"I knew it," said Cindy.

EVE SPENT the rest of her day drifting in and out of daydreams
about her and Nick and what the future held for them. Then,
when her last class was over, she brushed the snow from her
car and began the drive home. Cindy had only partially been
right. The snow, which had been flying most of the day, was
nearly gone from the roads, but as she topped the ridge leading
away from town, it began falling once more.

By the time she made it to Tazewell, the world was white
again, including the roads. Cautiously, she proceeded south
toward home.

When the farm came into view, she breathed a sigh of
relief. But her heart nearly stopped when Andi appeared on
the road, just below her house. It was as if she had come out of
nowhere.

"Are you hurt?" Eve jumped out of the car in a panic and
rushed to Andi's side.

"I'm fine." The girl stood and wiped the snow from her pants.

"What are you doing out here?" Eve cried, looking her over. She had only nudged her with the front of the car.

"Really," Andi said. "It's my fault. I should have been paying attention."

Eve put a hand to her heart and let out a sigh of relief. "Come on. Let's get you to the house."

They drove up to Eve's place and went inside. Eve found a couple of logs and started a fire.

"What were you doing out there in the cold? You could have frozen to death," Eve asked as she put a teakettle on the stove.

"I like to go for walks," Andi said. "It helps me clear my head. It wasn't snowing when I started."

Based on what Eve had seen on the drive home, that sounded plausible.

"Still, I'm glad I found you when I did, even though I nearly ran you over. God knows the weather can turn here in the blink of an eye."

When the teakettle whistled, Eve found two cups, dropped a bag in each one, filled them with water, and then set them aside to steep.

"Give that a couple of minutes and it'll be ready. Do you prefer honey?"

"Yes please," Andi said as the color returned to her cheeks. "I think I'm all right, really."

"I know. But it will make me feel better if you drink this. At least you can warm up before I take you home." She handed a cup of tea to Andi as she looked at Nick's place.

"He's not home," Andi informed her. "Saw his truck pull out a few minutes before you showed up."

"Oh," Eve said, turning back to her.

"Is he your friend?" Andi asked, sipping the tea.

"Yes, he is," Eve smiled. "A very good friend."

"Boyfriend?"

Eve's eyes went up.

"I'm thirteen," Andi said as if she had years of experience in matters of the heart.

"Fair enough," Eve said, sitting in the chair nearest the door. "Yes, I suppose you could say he's my boyfriend, though it sounds a little weird now that I say it aloud. I always thought of girlfriends and boyfriends as teenagers or young adults. Sounds a little funny coming from someone in their thirties."

"Are you going to marry him?"

"You have a lot of questions, don't you?" Eve asked, nearly choking on her tea.

"I'm a kid. It's what I do best."

Eve thought about her question for a while before answering.

"Maybe," Eve answered finally.

Andi looked at her and smiled.

"He was over at the house once." Andi set her cup on the coffee table. "I didn't talk to him, but he seemed really nice."

"Oh, he is," Eve confirmed. "He's one of the nicest people I've ever met, and kind, and gentle, and…"

"Definitely going to get married," Andi said, grinning broadly.

They looked at each other and laughed.

When they had finished their tea, Eve asked if Andi wanted to call her mom.

"She's still at work," Andi informed her. "Do you mind taking me home?"

Eve went to the window and gazed down the hill toward the road. The snow had stopped, and she could see blacktop.

"Sure," she said, turning back to her. "Let me grab my coat."

"Thanks for doing this," said Andi, as they turned right out of the drive. "I don't know what I was thinking."

"Don't mention it," Eve replied. "Besides, don't feel too bad. I used to do stuff like that all the time when I was your age."

Eve glanced her way and noticed a faint grin.

"So, where did you say your house was?"

"There." Andi pointed up the hill to a Federal-style brick house. It was old, perhaps a century or more.

"Cool house." Eve pulled up into the drive.

"Yeah, it's not bad," Andi said indifferently. "Well, thanks again."

"You're welcome. Hey, tell your mom I'd like to meet her sometime. I feel like you've been to my house enough where she should at least know who I am."

"She does," said Andi as she exited the car. "I told her all about you. Well, bye."

Eve watched her until she disappeared into the house, then backed out of the drive and returned home. By then, Nick was back, so she called to see if he wanted to come over for dinner.

"How did you like driving in the snow?" he asked as he sat down at the kitchen table.

"A harrowing experience," she replied, raising her gaze. "There were a couple of times I thought I was going to slide off the road."

"The secret is to not hit the brakes, and if you start to slide, turn the wheel in the direction you're sliding. Then let gravity do the rest. Picked that one up from my old man years ago," he added, taking a bite of salad.

"I nearly killed poor Andi this afternoon," she said miserably as she went back to refill her plate with spaghetti. "She was out walking around in that weather. Can you believe that?"

"No. I can't," he replied with concern. "Where did you say this girl lived again? And why is she always showing up at your place?"

Eve shrugged. "She says she gets bored." She sat back down at the table. "But I think it has something to do with her home situation. Her dad isn't around, and her mom is always working or gone to the store or something. I told her this evening that I wanted to meet her mom, just so she knows who I am since Andi seems to find her way here a lot, and you know what she told me?"

Nick shook his head.

"She said she already told her mom all about me. What do you think she means by that?"

"Like I said before… teenagers."

THE NEXT DAY, Kathleen called Eve while she was at work and asked if she wanted to come over for dinner so they could catch up. Eve had been so busy with work, Nick, and then the holidays, that she had neglected Kathleen. But as they talked, it was apparent Kathleen had been busy too. She had been in Nashville at a beauty conference in December and had spoken with the bank about purchasing a building where she could open her own salon.

"That's so exciting." Eve congratulated her. "You'll have to tell me all about it. I have a class right now, but I'll come by after work and we can catch up."

Kathleen had the margaritas ready when Eve arrived, complete with a salt rim and limes, and music was playing from her new iPhone.

"It's like a cantina in here," said Eve as she stepped into the living room.

"Just trying to create a little ambience," said Kathleen in her strong Southern accent. "Here, have one." She handed Eve a margarita.

Eve took a sip and remembered the last time she'd drank too much. That was the night she had to call Nick to drive her home. She wouldn't let that happen again.

"Tell me more about this salon," Eve said as she found a comfortable seat.

"Well," Kathleen began, taking a seat on the couch. "I found this old building in New Tazewell, on Main Street. I think it used to be a knickknack shop or something. Anyway, it's for sale, and they're selling the place at next to nothing and I just thought now might be the right time to strike out on my own."

"What about Whitney? Won't she be upset?"

"I've known Whitney for a long time, and I've talked to her before about opening up my own place. That's why I was looking in New Tazewell instead of across the street from her. I know I'll only be ten minutes away, but around here it makes a difference."

"As long as she's okay with it, then I say go for it." Eve raised her glass. "To your new place and future success," she said, tapping her glass against Kathleen's.

They drank and talked and drank some more, but Eve took it slow. She was just finishing her first margarita when she told Kathleen about Nick. Kathleen knew about Nick, of course, as she and Eve spoke at least once a week, but she had heard nothing about the trip to Texas or them sleeping together.

"So is he good in bed?" Kathleen asked, her eyes ablaze with wonder.

"I'm not the type to kiss and tell," said Eve.

"Oh, come on. Since Brad and I split up, hearing about your love life is the only thing that keeps me going."

Eve considered telling her everything. After all, Kathleen was her best friend.

"I won't lie, the sex is great," said Eve, letting the alcohol do the talking. "And he definitely knows his way around the bedroom."

Kathleen's eyes widened. "And his…"

"Eve raised her hands and widened them to the point Kathleen's mouth fell open.

"I knew it," she said, rising to her feet to get a refill. "I knew I should have gone after him when I had the chance." She paused. "No offense."

"None taken," Eve said. Kathleen was not in the same league as Nick.

Kathleen returned a minute later with fresh drinks. Again, Eve sipped conservatively as she felt the buzz kick in.

"Do you think there's something there with him, or is it sex only?"

Eve hesitated. She wasn't the type of woman who was only interested in sex. There had to be more to it than that. She enjoyed the idea of loving someone and being loved, and in Nick, she had found someone who shared those same feelings. "I think it's more than that," she admitted. "Nick is sweet and caring and—"

"Oh God. You're in love with him, aren't you?"

Eve dropped her gaze as she felt her face get hot.

"I don't know," she answered truthfully. "I've not been with many men, so I don't have a ton of experience with these things, but I've never met anyone like him before."

Kathleen became instantly sober as the conversation had turned serious.

"What about his family? Is he over that whole thing?"

"I don't think anyone ever gets over something like that." Eve ignored Kathleen's unintended insensitivity. "But he does his best to deal with it. Still, I can't help but think he's still holding on to something. I'll catch him staring into space sometimes, and I know he's thinking about them."

"Does that bother you?"

"No. Not entirely," she answered. "But I wonder if he'll ever be able to move on."

Kathleen downed another drink, but Eve stopped at two. Any more, and she'd have to call Nick again. So instead of focusing the conversation on her relationship, which made her want to drink more, she switched gears.

"You know a lot of people around here, right?" She set her glass on the table.

"Unfortunately," she said, raising an eyebrow.

Eve stifled a laugh. "There's this girl that I keep running into. I was hoping you could tell me something about her family."

"Girl?"

"Yeah, a teenager. She lives a couple of miles down the road from me. Her name is Andi, with an *i*."

"This girl got a last name?"

Suddenly, Eve realized she had never asked for her last name.

"I'm sure she does," Eve answered. "But I don't know what

it is. She and her mother live in the old house on Calloway Road that looks like it was built during the Civil War.

"You mean the old Ousley place?"

"No." The Ousley place was the one Nick told her about, the one that was abandoned. "It has two chimneys, made entirely of brick... Oh, and it has a giant oak in the front yard with a split down the middle. Maybe it was struck by lightning or something."

"Yeah, that's the Ousley place," Kathleen confirmed. "But no one lives there. That old place has been abandoned for years. Are you sure that's where she lives?"

Now that Eve thought of it, she wasn't sure. She had dropped Andi off and had watched her walk inside, but after that, she could have gone anywhere. Then she realized Andi's home situation might be worse than she thought. Perhaps she was ashamed to show Eve where she really lived.

"You know what? Maybe you're right. It was snowing so hard when I dropped her off, I was probably looking at the wrong house."

CHAPTER 14

THE OUSLEY HOUSE

Weeks passed and winter faded, giving way to the warm breezes of spring. Life for Eve had become so hectic there was rarely a moment she wasn't thinking about work or her mother or both. Since Christmas, Nancy's condition had deteriorated to the point she was having difficulty remembering who she was. Eve and her sisters were astounded by the rapid decline even though it mimicked their grandmother years earlier.

Nick was as supportive as could be, comforting Eve when she needed it, being a shoulder to lean on and cry on. Mostly though, he was there to sit and listen and love.

One morning while Eve was at work, Nick drove to the coffeehouse. He knew she'd been having a hard time lately, so he wanted to do something to raise her spirits. While he wasn't a man of grand gestures, he'd been around long enough to realize it was the little things that made the greatest impact.

"Well, well, well," Joyce greeted Nick as he walked through

the door and strolled to the counter. "Look what the cat dragged in."

It had been a few days since his last visit, and although Eve had broken the routine that had for so long dominated his life, there were pieces he still held on to.

"Morning, Joyce." He gave her a grin. "How about a couple of white-chocolate mochas and a doughnut with chocolate icing?"

"Coming right up." She began preparing his drinks but kept talking. "You know, I never thought I'd see the day when you'd come in here and order anything other than black coffee," she said as she mixed the espresso with hot milk.

"People change." Nick leaned against the counter.

"Yes, they certainly do. I assume the other drink is for Ms. Gentry?"

"That's right," he said. "She's been having a rough time lately, and I was hoping to surprise her this morning."

"Is everything okay?" Joyce's brow formed a tight line over her eyes.

"Her mother is ill," Nick said. "Alzheimer's. Unfortunately, she's not getting any better." He felt strange talking about it as if he were qualified to discuss her condition.

"I'm sorry to hear that," Joyce said thoughtfully. "Does that mean Eve won't be sticking around?"

"I don't know." Nick suddenly felt miserable. The question had caught him off guard. Summer was fast approaching, and Eve would have several months to spend at home if she needed to, but her moving back would be an altogether different story. And one he was not prepared for.

When the drinks were ready, Joyce handed them to Nick and told him to let Eve know she would pray for her and her family.

At the university, Nick took the elevator to the third floor and walked down to Eve's office, running into Cindy along the way.

"She's not in her office this morning," Cindy told him as she eyed the mochas. "Professor Owens is out sick today, so Eve is filling in for her. She's delivering a lecture in Duke Hall, just across the way." She gestured with her hand, then glanced at her watch. "It should let out soon."

Since Nick had begun seeing Eve, he had become quite familiar with the layout of the campus. He took her to lunch twice a week, and when the weather was nice, they enjoyed an occasional stroll to the park. Nick thanked Cindy and found the path that led to the steps of Duke Hall.

He slipped through an open door and stopped in the atrium as the sound of Eve's voice reverberating in the great hall brought a smile to his face. Peering through a small opening in the door, he watched as she delivered a lecture on nineteenth-century literature. He marveled at her intelligence, her confidence, and the way she seemed at ease in front of a crowd. She was all the things he wasn't, and for a brief second, he wondered what he had done to deserve someone like her.

When the lecture was over, Nick slid out of the way, letting the auditorium empty. Once the students departed, he slipped inside and made his way to the front of the room, where Eve was packing up her things.

"Stirring lecture," he said as he approached.

Eve looked up at the sound of his voice. "Nick." She smiled, surprised to see him. "What have you brought for me today?" she asked as she descended the stage.

"White-chocolate mocha," he told her. "Oh, and one of those doughnuts you like," he added, producing the small box he'd been hiding behind his back.

"You shouldn't have." Eve cocked her head to one side. "But I'm glad you did. Today has been a bit of a disaster. Professor Owens—"

"I heard. I ran into Cindy in the hall."

"So what brings you out this way? I thought you had to go see Marjorie this morning."

"That was the plan, but she canceled at the last minute. I think John has the flu."

"That's too bad. I hope he's all right." Eve found an open seat at the back, and they sat down and enjoyed their drinks while she did her best to relax.

"I was watching you through the window," Nick told her as he finished the last of his drink. "You're quite good."

"You're too kind," she said.

"Seriously. You've got a gift. There's no way I could stand up there in front of all those kids and do what you do. It's quite impressive."

"Thank you." She knew Nick well enough to know he was sincere. "It means a lot to hear you say that." She took another sip. "You know, if someone would have told me two years ago that right now I'd be sitting in a lecture hall in Tennessee, enjoying coffee with a handsome man after having just delivered a lecture on Mark Twain, I would have told them they were crazy." She laughed.

"And yet here we are," he said.

"Yes. Here we are," she repeated. Her gaze drifted to Nick, who had set his upon the stage.

Eve waited a while before speaking again. "I got a call this morning," she said, clearing her throat. "From Mel."

"What did Mel have to say?" he asked carefully.

"Mom had a fall yesterday. She lost her balance and fell on the front steps."

"Is she okay?" he asked, looking worried.

"She's a little banged up, but she'll survive," Eve replied.

Nick sensed there was more.

Eve fought back the tears as she struggled to find a voice. "She also had a doctor visit a couple of days ago, and she found out that the Alzheimer's has gotten worse. Nick, she's dying," Eve said through blurry eyes.

Nick had a history with death, so he felt the anxiety swell inside him when she said the word.

"I don't know what to say," he breathed as he struggled to process. "How long?"

"A few months, give or take." Tears streamed down her otherwise perfect face, which was more than Nick could take. He'd shouldered the load of misery and pain with the loss of his wife and daughter, but to see someone else suffering, someone he cared for, was in many ways worse.

He took the cup from her, set it on the ground, then circled his arms around her and held her as she cried. Something was comforting in the release of tears, as if it had a way of renewing the soul, something Nick understood all too well.

When Eve was out of tears, she reached into her purse and grabbed a tissue, dried her eyes, and made a comment about ruining her makeup.

"You look beautiful," he said tenderly as he wiped away the last of the tears from her face.

Eve smiled. Even with red, blurry eyes and a tear-streaked face, she was the most beautiful woman he'd ever laid eyes on. He wanted to kiss her and make all her troubles go away, but he knew that was impossible. Still, his instinct to protect was undeniable, and as he leaned forward, kissing her gently on the forehead, he felt helpless.

"Hey, I was thinking," Nick said as they separated.

"About what?"

"Why don't we ride out to the Ousley place this weekend? I promised you a few months ago we'd check it out, but the weather turned, then we got busy with the holidays, and—"

"When?"

"Saturday, if you're up for it."

"Yeah. I'd like that," she replied happily as a smile returned to her face.

ON SATURDAY MORNING AFTER BREAKFAST, Nick wrangled the horses while Eve dressed. The Ousley place was on the other side of the ridge, near the lake. Nick had driven by it a few times but had never attempted the journey on horseback.

"I'm glad we picked today," said Eve, marveling at the beautiful morning they had before them.

"The weather should be near perfect most of the day," he commented, turning his gaze skyward as a pair of wispy clouds drifted overhead.

He helped Eve get one foot into the stirrup. Once she had lifted herself, Nick did the same, and they began the journey toward the Ousley house. As they rode, Eve thought about the last time she had seen Andi. It was that cold, snowy day when she'd nearly run her over with the car. Since then, she hadn't been by, and she wondered if Andi had simply gotten busy with life, or she was avoiding her.

As they topped the ridge, rather than descend the other side toward the lake like they had done the previous fall, Nick led them across the back of the ridge, through the thickest part of the forest, until they came to the end of the trail.

"It's just there." He pointed ahead to a clearing beyond the trees.

Eve craned her neck to have a better look. They were on the other side of the brick house, opposite the road, but even from that angle, Eve recognized it as being the same place where she had dropped Andi off weeks before.

"I've been here before," Eve commented as they eased toward the house. "This is where Andi had me drop her off the day it snowed."

"Why would she have you drop her off here?" Nick mused aloud.

Eve shrugged, now pulling up alongside Nick and Shadow. "She made it sound like this was where she lived."

When they got close enough to see inside, it was clear no one had lived in the Ousley house in years. Two windows were broken, and there was a hole in the roof the size of a Volkswagen.

They moved ahead a little farther, but something stirring in the tall grass spooked the horses. And no matter how hard Nick tried to convince Shadow to go forward, she refused.

"All right." He glanced over at Eve. "Let's tie them up here so they don't run off."

"Everything all right?" she asked as Cinnamon suddenly felt tense beneath her.

"Fine," he answered. "Must be those butterflies." He nodded at a pair of Monarchs fluttering nearby. "Horses are afraid of butterflies."

Eve had never heard of that before, but she found it quite amusing.

Once the horses were tied up, Nick helped Eve down, and they set off for the house on foot.

"This place was originally built by Jacob Sharp in 1835," he began, as though he was giving a lecture in local history. "After the Civil War, he fell on hard times and sold the place to Jacob Ousley. It's been in his family ever since."

"You'd make an excellent history teacher," she said, smiling at him.

"I wouldn't go that far." He laughed. "But local history does fascinate me."

"It's such a beautiful place." Eve scanned the property. "Why was it abandoned?"

"Depends on who you ask," Nick responded as he mounted the porch. "Some say that when the last resident died, there was no one else to pass it down to."

"And others?" Eve asked curiously as she joined him.

"Well, that's where folks like you come in." He grinned and pushed open the front door. "Many think the reason no one lives here anymore is that it's haunted."

Eve felt her stomach tighten as the door creaked open.

"Careful," Nick warned as they stepped inside. "It's still early in the year, but there could be a snake or two."

Eve wasn't a fan of snakes, having nearly been bitten by a rattlesnake when she was a girl. As she followed Nick through the house, she stayed close, keeping her eyes peeled.

The air inside the house was dank and stagnant, the light dim, and by the droppings on the floor, it was clear the house wasn't completely unoccupied.

"Why do you think she came in here?" Eve whispered, her thoughts drifting back to Andi as they made their way to the foot of the central staircase.

"Who?" Nick asked as he looked up toward the second floor.

"Andi."

Nick shrugged. "Maybe she was doing the same thing we're

doing. Ghost hunting." He laughed. But it was clear Eve was in search of a plausible explanation. "Kids are always coming up here, trying to prove this place is haunted," he said, defending his answer. "Or maybe she lives in one of the rundown homes nearby and didn't want you to see it."

"That's what I told Kathleen."

"There are some pretty rough places around here," Nick said as he carefully ascended the steps. "Watch your step." He pointed to a soft spot where the wood had rotted through. "Some families in the area are extremely poor. I don't know anything about Andi's home situation, but if I had to guess, I'd say she was just embarrassed."

Eve felt better, but there was still that nagging feeling inside her that there was more to the story. As they searched the upstairs, Nick and Eve went through each room, both commenting on what a shame it was that such a lovely house had fallen into disrepair.

"I bet this place was quite something in its day," said Nick as they entered the bedroom with the hole in the roof. "Can you imagine what life must have been like back then?"

Eve had always had an active imagination, so as she closed her eyes, she could feel the place come alive around her. Whether she saw a spirit or not, it didn't matter because she could feel the energy of generations.

When she opened her eyes, Nick stood with his back to her as he examined an old bookshelf.

Eve went to the window and gazed out over the property, and as she did, she caught sight of someone standing at the edge of the woods. "Hey Nick?" she said, unable to remove her gaze.

"Yeah?"

"I think someone is watching us." She squinted, trying to make the person out.

"Where?" He rushed to her side.

"There." Eve pointed to a clump of trees. "Right there."

Nick looked to where she was pointing but saw nothing.

Before Nick could say another word, Eve had retreated from the window and was making her way back down the steps.

"Eve, wait!" Nick shouted as he gave chase.

In a flash, Eve had descended the steps and was back outside. She jumped off the porch, veered right, and set off for the trees where she had seen the figure. By the time Nick caught up with her, she was standing with one hand on her hip while she ran the other through her hair.

"I know I saw someone," she said, feeling as though she was losing her mind. "I think… I think it was Andi."

"Are you sure?"

"I think so. But how would she know we were out here? And why would she be following us?"

"Never know," he replied, unfazed. "Perhaps she saw the horses and wanted to have a closer look."

"But that would mean she lives close by, right? Do you mind if we have a look around the property? It will make me feel much better."

Nick reluctantly agreed.

They waded through the knee-deep grass until they reached the edge of the field. Beyond that lay shrubs and thick vegetation that neither of them wanted to negotiate.

"Maybe those trailers down there?" Eve pointed to a small field where a half dozen rusted mobile homes sat close together. "Perhaps she lives in one of those."

Nick nodded along. "Well, mystery solved," he said as he turned back.

"You don't want to find out?" she asked.

"I don't see a way down there, do you?"

Eve scanned the area, but there was no trail and no safe way to descend the hill.

"I suppose not," she said, looking disappointed. "There has to be a road somewhere."

Nick scanned the horizon and found the lake. Once he'd gotten his bearings, he said, "Brantley Road, I believe. It connects to the highway. That should take you right to them."

"Brantley Road," repeated Eve, committing it to memory.

BY THE TIME they made their way back to the farm, daylight was fading fast. It was spring, and the days grew longer, but the air was still cool in the evening, especially after sunset, so they were eager to get in before dark.

Once the horses were taken care of, Nick closed the gate and walked Eve back to her place.

"I'd like it if you would stay the night," she said as she eased toward her porch.

"I could do that," he replied, taking her by the hands. "But I need to get out of these clothes and shower first. I've got a couple of steaks we could put on the grill, or..."

"That sounds nice," she said. "I'll grab a shower and prepare a salad. Come over when you're ready."

Nick went home and set the steaks on the counter to rest while he went for a shower. After he cleaned up, he grabbed the steaks and a bottle of wine and descended the hill.

"Thank you for taking me out to the house today. I had fun."

"Sorry we didn't see any ghosts," he said playfully.

"That's all right," she replied. "Maybe another time. But at least we made a memory," she added, looking on the bright side.

"To memories." Nick raised his glass and tapped it against Eve's.

They drank slowly, but they were in no hurry. Besides, they both knew where the night would lead, so there was no added pressure. They had made it past the awkward phase when neither of them knew how to act around the other. Now it came easy, and they were both thankful for that.

THE FOLLOWING week was plagued with wet weather. Rain moved in and hung around for days, to the point the creek at the end of the drive had swelled outside its banks and covered the road. Finally, the rain ended, and the sun returned. After being so long confined inside with work, Eve was eager to get out and explore. With spring in full swing, the air was warm, the grass an emerald green, and the trees were in bloom.

Rather than burden Nick with chasing ghosts, Eve set out to find Brantley Road on her own. She knew approximately where it was located, but she had never been out that far on her own, and she wandered the countryside for the better part of an hour before she found it. At the end of the narrow road sat a half dozen rusted trailers that looked as if they had been sitting there for decades.

As she ground the car to a halt, she wondered how anyone could live there. There were one or two old cars in the driveways, but they were missing tires or engines or both, and as she got out and proceeded on foot, she thought she had struck out again.

"Looking for me?" a voice called out behind her.

"Andi," Eve said, spinning around. She put a hand to her heart as she caught her breath. "I was just—"

"You're probably wondering what I'm doing down here," she said as if she could read Eve's mind. "Until we can get the house fixed up, Mom says we have to stay here." She turned her attention to the single-wide trailer behind her. "It's not so bad though," she continued, putting on a brave face. "My best friend lives there." She pointed to the last home in the row, the one with light blue siding. "I'd invite you in, but Mom doesn't like for me to have people over when she's not at home." She turned back to Eve.

"That's all right," said Eve. "Is your mother at work?"

Andi nodded.

"And what does she do?" Eve inquired carefully.

Andi shrugged. "Something to do with numbers, I think. I'm not really sure," she said hopelessly.

They walked on a little farther, and as they did, Eve realized not a single light burned in any of the homes.

"A bit of a ghost town around here, isn't it?" she joked, trying to lighten the mood.

Andi swung her gaze to Eve. "Something like that." Andi walked on a few more steps and paused as they neared the road. "Why'd you come down here, anyway?"

"I wanted to invite you and your mom to dinner this Saturday night at my place," she said, thinking fast. "Do you think she would be interested?"

Andi stiffened. "Um... I'll have to check with her," she

replied, looking troubled. "She normally likes to rest on the weekends… you know, after a hard week of work and all."

"I understand," said Eve. "Then what about a night during the week? I'll let her pick."

Andi didn't answer right away and appeared to be thinking. "Like I said, I'll ask her," she said politely as she forced a smile.

After a few seconds of silence, they turned and headed back up the road.

"You know, if there's anything you want to tell me, I'm a good listener," Eve offered, now confident Andi was hiding something.

Andi gave a crooked smile, then dropped it. "Thanks," she said. "The counselors at school used to say the same thing."

"And how do you like school? Are you a good student?"

"I do okay." She frowned. "But I like to read."

"Really?" Eve said. "You know, I'm a teacher—well, professor."

"And what do you teach?"

"English," Eve answered proudly.

"That's my favorite subject," said Andi, her eyes lighting up. "I just love to read."

"Me too," said Eve as they pressed on. "Do you have a favorite author?"

"No. I like everything, except horror." Andi winced a little.

"Well, the next time you're around the house, I'll have to show you my collection of books. You could borrow them if you like."

"That'd be great," said Andi.

They walked on in silence until they reached Andi's home.

"Well, it was good to see you again," Andi said as she reached for the railing to the stairs. "But I really should get back inside."

Eve backed away as she opened the door and slipped inside. "Remember what I said?" she reminded her. "Any night of the week is fine." Eve turned and went for her car, and as she reached it, she gave one last look to Andi's home. Above the door, she noticed a sign that read THE OWENS. *Ah-hah*, she thought. Now she had a last name.

A WEEK PASSED, and although Eve had left the invitation open for Andi and her mother to come to supper, she would not hold her breath. After all, Andi seemed to come and go like the seasons, and as far as Eve was concerned, she wasn't convinced the girl had a mother at all.

With another day of teaching behind her, she changed into sweats and a T-shirt, pulled her hair into a ponytail, and sat down to a bowl of soup and half a ham and cheese. But before she could take the first bite, the doorbell rang. *Strange*, she thought as she rose and crossed the living room floor. Nick never used the doorbell.

Instinctively, she looked through the peephole, and what she found on the other side shocked her.

"Andi, what a nice surprise," Eve said as she eased open the door. Her eyes drifted from Andi to the woman standing behind her. She was around Eve's age, perhaps a few years older and an inch shorter, with soft brown eyes and sandy-blond hair. Despite her having a teenager, she appeared young for her age.

"Eve, meet my mother, Liza," said Andi.

"You do exist," Eve said, shaking the woman's hand. "I mean, it's so nice to finally meet you. Please come in. I was just sitting down to supper. Would you like some?"

"We wouldn't want to impose," Liza said as she stepped into the living room.

"You're not imposing," Eve replied. "I always make more than I need. Trust me, there's plenty to go around."

"Sorry for dropping in like this. I typically work late, but tonight I finished up early. Andi's been begging me all week to drop by and pay you a visit, so…"

"Well, I'm glad you did," said Eve, overjoyed. "It gets awfully lonely here on the farm, so any chance I get to have company is a treat."

Eve showed them into the kitchen, and as they ate soup and sandwiches, Eve couldn't help but feel she had known them her whole life.

"You have a lovely home," Liza commented as her gaze drifted from the kitchen to the living room.

"Thank you," replied Eve proudly. But she caught herself and dialed back the smile. "I've only been here since last fall."

"New to the area?"

"Yes—well, sort of. I moved here last summer… from Texas… that's where I'm from originally."

"That must have been hard—moving so far away?"

"Yes and no," said Eve, stopping short of burdening them with the details of her divorce. "But I really like it here. I have a good job at the university, and everyone is friendly."

"And she has a boyfriend," Andi chimed in.

Eve looked mortified, but she quickly got over it.

"Is this the man on the hill you were telling me about?" Liza asked Andi.

Andi nodded.

"His name is Nick," said Eve. "Nick Sullivan. I believe you know him. Andi said he was at your house once."

Liza's gaze shifted from Andi to Eve. "Yes, I believe he was... to fix the sink or something. He seemed like a nice man." "Yes, he is," replied Eve. "So Andi tells me you work with numbers. What exactly do you do?" She was eager to steer the conversation in a new direction.

Liza shot a look at Andi, who nodded as if granting her permission to speak.

"I'm an accountant," she said. "For the city."

"Oh, that must be exciting. I've never been a numbers person myself. I've always done better with words. The whole right-brain thing, I suppose." Eve chuckled but quickly killed the smile as no one else found her attempt at humor funny. "I'm glad we finally got to meet. Andi's been over to the house a few times, and I wanted to make sure you knew who I was."

The woman shot a glance in Andi's direction, causing her to drop her gaze.

"I hope that's all right?" Eve asked, sensing trouble.

"Fine," said Liza with a smile as she turned back to Eve.

When dinner was over, Eve and Liza sat in the kitchen talking while Andi watched TV.

"Is everything okay with Andi?" Eve asked as they set the dishes in the sink.

"What do you mean?"

"I don't know. Sometimes she seems like she has a lot on her mind. I told her I was here if she ever needed someone to talk to. I hope that's all right?"

She smiled and nodded as her eyes drifted to Andi. "Ever since her father left, she hasn't been the same," she explained as she turned back. "If I'm honest, neither of us have."

"Do you mind if I ask what happened?" Eve asked delicately.

"He was taken from us," she explained, her countenance

growing dark. "It was like he was here one minute and gone the next."

Eve remained silent, hoping she would elaborate, but when she didn't, Eve said, "I know what you mean."

"You lost someone too?"

"Yes," Eve said with a nod. "My dad. He died last January."

"The pain never really goes away, does it?"

"I suppose not," said Eve, trying to be strong. "But I like to think he's still here with me, in my heart." She put a hand to her chest.

"I feel the same way about Andi's father," she said. "Sometimes he feels close enough to touch, but others..." Her voice faded as she dropped her gaze.

"I'm sorry." Eve handed her a tissue. "I didn't mean to upset you."

"Don't give it another thought," she said, drying her eyes. "Sometimes it's good to let the tears out. Otherwise, I think we'd all explode, wouldn't we?"

"I suppose you're right," Eve said, finding a smile.

"Well, I really should get home. It's getting late and Andi has school tomorrow. Thank you." She looked at Eve. "It's been a long time since I've done anything like this."

"You're welcome," said Eve, rising to her feet. "And you're welcome in my house anytime, both of you."

"Thank you," said Liza.

EVE DIDN'T SEE Liza after that, but at least she knew she was real, and Andi wasn't living alone. Still, there was something odd about them.

Another month passed, and as spring break drew near, Eve

was planning to use the time to go home for a few days. Mel and Cassie had done an admirable job of holding down the fort, but Eve needed to be there.

But before the week was over, she received a call from the dean of the English department, saying she wanted to speak with Eve in her office.

"Do come in," said Dean Robbins with a smile as she removed her glasses and set them at the corner of her desk.

Eve slipped inside the room and made herself comfortable. "You wanted to see me?" she asked, feeling suddenly nervous.

"Yes, I did, and thank you for being so prompt," she said in a high-spirited voice. "As I'm sure you're aware, another academic year is quickly drawing to a close. I hope you've enjoyed your first year with us."

"Yes ma'am." Eve straightened herself in the chair. "It's been, well, a dream come true, if you don't mind my saying."

"I don't mind at all. In fact, I remember saying those exact words at the end of my first year, though heavens, that's been the better part of three decades now," she said as her eyes drifted to the ceiling. "The other professors and I were talking the other evening," she continued, clearing her expression. "And we were wondering if you would be interested in returning next year."

"Really?" Until now, Eve wasn't certain where she stood.

"Your students love you, Professor Gentry." She crossed her arms and leaned against the bookshelf. "And you're quite proficient behind the podium. My opinion, for what it's worth, is you have a long career in education ahead of you, and if you're open to the idea, I'd like that to be here."

Eve wanted to say yes right away, but she caught herself.

"Is something the matter?"

"No ma'am. I mean, yes—well, maybe. It's just my mother, she's sick."

"I'm sorry to hear that," she replied sincerely. "I wasn't aware."

"I've kept it a secret," Eve confessed. "I didn't want it to impede my work."

"And I admire you for that. It's difficult enough to move so far away. Mix that with a parent who is ill, and…"

"I'm using the time off next week to fly home and check on her. Then I'll have the summer, and…"

"Take your time," she said. "I don't need an answer today. Even if it means getting back to me this summer when you have a better read on things. Ultimately, the job is yours if you want it, and if not, well, I completely understand."

With that, Eve thanked Dean Robbins and returned to her office. She sat alone with the door closed for a long time and stared out the window. She had come so far, but it seemed every time she advanced a step, life knocked her back two.

CHAPTER 15

CROSSROADS

On Friday night after dinner, Eve began packing. With her mother's condition worsening by the day, she was reluctant to put off the trip until summer for fear it would be too late.

Then, when she was at a stopping point, she went to talk to Nick.

"I could go with you," he offered as they sat on his porch sipping sweet tea.

It was only ten o'clock, but the sun was bright and the air warm.

"I appreciate the offer, but I'll be fine," Eve reassured him. "Besides, this is something I need to do on my own. You understand, don't you?"

Nick understood, but that didn't prevent him from being disappointed. He wanted to press her, to make her understand it would be more complicated than she expected and that she would inevitably need a shoulder to cry on, but he held his tongue.

"I'm going to miss you," he said glumly.

"I'll miss you as well." She reached for his hand. "But I'll only be a week. And with that new order you got, you'll be so busy you won't even realize I'm gone."

He knew she was only trying to make things better. Being without her for a day, an hour, even a minute, was agonizing enough, but a whole week was difficult for him to wrap his mind around. She had become a part of him, woven into the fabric of his life. Sure, there'd be work, and hard work at that, but his mind would be on her the entire time, counting down the minutes until she returned.

"Can I at least drive you to the airport?" he asked, searching for some consolation.

"I'd be upset if you didn't." Eve leaned over and kissed him as if they had been together for years. It was comfortable now, easy, but the spark she had felt when their lips touched the first time was still there, electric as ever.

When they finished their tea, Eve returned home to resume packing. Five o'clock would come early, and she didn't want to leave anything to the last minute. As the sun went down, she slapped together a ham and cheese for dinner, watched TV for a while, then turned in early.

Nick, on the other hand, stayed up well past midnight, worrying about Eve.

Morning came, and the alarm clock pulled Eve from a dream so vivid she couldn't shake it as she got ready to leave the house. She was sitting on a bench at the back of her father's workshop. It was nearly dusk, the sun inching its way toward the horizon. It was a memory from just after the divorce.

"Everything will be okay," her dad said to her as he draped an arm across her shoulders. "You'll get to see what you're made of now. And I think you're made of all the right stuff."

"I don't know, daddy," she said feebly, staring off into the distance. "I feel like a ship with no sail."

"That's natural," he replied lovingly. "You've been through a traumatic experience."

"But what about mama? When I told her the divorce was final, she looked at me as if I had somehow disappointed her."

"Your mother is a complicated woman," Frank said. "She loves you more than you will ever know. Sometimes, she just doesn't know the right thing to say to you, and it ends up coming out all wrong. The two of you remind me of my two sisters." He sported a smile. "They used to be at each other all the time about one thing or another. Then one day they sat down and had an adult conversation and concluded that they were more similar than they realized. I suspect the same thing will happen with you and Mom someday."

"Don't be so sure," she said.

"Have I ever been wrong before?"

Eve tried to stifle a smile, but it was no use, and as she rolled her eyes, she thought about how many times her father had been right over the years. It was something of a superpower.

A knock on the door pulled Eve from her daydream. It was Nick, bright-eyed, ready to help load luggage.

"Is this all?" he asked, finding a single suitcase and a carry-on bag.

"Just the basics," she told him as she went to the kitchen to make coffee. "If I need anything else, I can get it while I'm there."

"Okay." Nick grabbed the suitcase and carry-on. He loaded them into the truck and returned as Eve poured two cups of coffee.

"Just the way you like it," she said, handing him a cup.

Nick smiled, perhaps too much, but he was hanging on every word now.

"What is it?" she asked, seeing that he was thinking about something.

"Nothing… just thinking about the first time we met."

Eve smiled.

"It's funny how life leads us to places we never thought we would be," he said philosophically. "If I hadn't been at the coffeehouse that morning, or if Sam's class hadn't run long, or if I hadn't agreed to make that delivery, you and I may never have met."

Eve rarely dwelt on such things, but it was clear Nick had given this a great deal of thought.

"But we did," she said happily. "Whether it was fate or coincidence or divine intervention, you and I were at the right place at the right time."

Nick stared longingly into her eyes as the emotions swirled inside him. Then, when he had collected his thoughts and steadied himself, he said, "I love you."

She looked up from her coffee, stunned. His comment had caught her off guard. "I love you too," she said, finding a voice. "You've never said that before."

Nick raised his hand and brushed back the hair from her eyes, tucking it behind her ear. "I should have said it months ago. I suppose I felt it that first day, but only now have I been able to muster the courage to say it."

Again, Eve felt a rush as Nick leaned in and pressed his lips against hers, parting long enough to tell her once more that he loved her.

Their time was up. Eve locked up, handed Nick the keys, and they moved to the truck.

"And you promise to watch over things while I'm away?"

"Cross my heart." He smiled and traced an X on his chest, and it was so adorable Eve felt her own heart squeeze.

She took one more look at the house before she got in the truck; and then they sped off down the road.

Nick dropped her off at the terminal and watched until she had disappeared beyond the glass doors. As he pulled away, he wondered how he would manage without her for an entire week.

THE FLIGHT WAS UNEVENTFUL, which was precisely the way Eve wanted it, and by the time she stepped off the plane, she was more anxious than ever to get home.

"How is she?" were the first words out of Eve's mouth as she found her sisters waiting in the terminal. This time, Cassie was there. Eve frowned.

"Not well," said Mel, giving it to her straight. "It's good you came when you did."

Eve had used the time during the flight to prepare herself for the worst. Things had happened so quickly with her father that she hadn't had time to think, but now, even though things were rushing, she could at least die a little every day rather than all at once. But the longer she thought about that, the more she wondered which was worse.

Eve grabbed her bags and found Mel's SUV, and off they went. Two hours went by quickly, but mainly because the anticipation of seeing her mother was weighing heavily on her. She and her sisters chatted a bit and tried to keep the conversation light, but no matter how hard they tried, it inevitably drifted back to their mother.

"Listen," said Mel, pulling her to the side as Cassie went

into the house. "Don't get upset if she doesn't remember you. Her memory comes and goes like the tides now. Some days are better than others, but—"

"Mel, I got this." Eve put on a brave face.

At the house, she stepped into a familiar silence, the same as just after her father's funeral. Before that day, she never knew the silence could be so loud.

"Mom?" She searched the living room and kitchen.

"Here." Nancy appeared in the hallway.

If possible, she had aged another ten years since Christmas. Eve pretended not to notice, but the pain she saw in her mother's eyes nearly broke her.

They embraced for a long time, and Nancy remembered who she was, which came as a great comfort to Eve.

Cassie and Mel stayed out back on the covered porch while Eve and Nancy visited.

"How's Nick?" Nancy asked as she sat on the couch with a blanket.

"He's…" She hesitated, but only because she didn't have enough words to describe how wonderful he was. "He's great," she said finally, wishing he were there with her. "He told me he loved me this morning."

"That's wonderful, dear." Nancy looked happy. But her smile was short-lived as her mind became fuzzy. "Where's Frank?"

Eve stiffened. "Mama?"

"Go get your father," she demanded, her demeanor turning on a dime.

Eve got up and went to find Mel and Cassie.

"It's one of her episodes," said Mel, rushing to their mother's side.

Cassie held Nancy's hand and reassured her everything

would be all right while Eve stood at a distance, near the point of tears.

They took Nancy back to her room to rest, then joined Eve out on the porch.

"Is it like that all the time?" Eve asked, still shaken up.

"A half dozen times a day," said Cassie sadly.

"That's why we called in hospice," whispered Mel, closing the door behind her. "With my work schedule and Cassie busy with the kids, we don't have the time to be here every minute of the day."

Eve felt guilty for not being closer to home. When she'd left the previous summer, getting as far away from Athens, Texas, was the only thing she cared about, but now that the situation had changed, she wanted nothing more than to be close so she could pitch in and help.

"I'm coming home for the summer."

Cassie and Mel looked at one another.

"Is that what you want?" asked Mel, looking skeptical.

Eve nodded, though not with as much enthusiasm as her sisters would have wanted.

"And what about Nick?" Cassie asked, saying what Mel was already thinking.

"He and I discussed it before I left. He understands."

Mel wasn't convinced. "Listen, Eve," she began, choosing her words carefully. "I know you mean well, but your life isn't here anymore. You moved away to start a new life, and I think it's the best thing that's ever happened to you. Don't let guilt drag you back to a place where you don't want to be."

Eve thought about her sister's words for a long time. Mel had always been the voice of reason in her life. Even after the divorce, Mel was the one who told her to think big and look beyond the town of Athens and even the state of Texas.

"I agree with Mel," said Cassie, chiming in. "I know you and I have not always been the best of friends. God knows most of that is my fault, but you've made it out of this place. You're successful, and you've got a man who worships the ground you walk on. Take some time this summer if you choose. Mel and I would love to have you here, even if it is only for a couple of months. But don't give up everything because you feel a duty to be here."

Cassie's words hit her harder than Mel's, and as Eve tried to digest what they had told her, she couldn't help but feel she had come to a crossroads.

Late in the evening, they went in and had dinner.

The nurse from hospice came down around seven and prepared a plate for Nancy, then took it to her to eat.

An hour later, Mel checked on her, and after seeing she was asleep, shut the door and made her way to the living room.

"She's finally resting," said Mel, exhaling. Her eyes were red, tired, and faint lines had formed at the corners. "Today was a rough day, and I fear it's only going to get worse." She poured a glass of wine and sat down on the couch.

"We can't keep her here much longer," said Cassie, already halfway through her first glass. "We'll need to move her to a facility before long."

"How do you think that will go?" Eve asked, knowing how stubborn her mother could be.

"She won't go without a fight." Mel let the alcohol slide down her throat. "Mama's always been a fighter."

"But it's for the best, right?" Eve wanted to be sure there was no other way.

Her sisters nodded in unison.

They sat in the living room until after eleven. It was nice for the three of them to spend time together and be sisters again, even if it was under less-than-ideal circumstances. It reminded Eve of summer nights when she was a girl when she and her sisters would have slumber parties in the backyard beneath the stars.

When they had drunk all the wine and exhaustion had overtaken them, they said good night. Then each set off in search of a bed.

Cassie slept in her old room while Mel took the couch. Eve set up in the guest room, and once she had closed the door, she grabbed her cell and called Nick. It was late, but she was hoping he was still awake.

"Everything okay?" he asked, relieved to hear her voice.

Eve hesitated. "No," she finally said, trying to hold it together.

"Do you need me to fly down there? I could be on a plane first thing in the morning."

Eve knew he was serious, but she told him she could manage on her own.

"If you change your mind…"

"That means a great deal to me." She kept her voice to a whisper. "This is harder than I imagined. Mom had an episode today while we were talking, and she started asking for my dad. I thought I was ready, but…" A lump formed in Eve's throat.

"I'm sorry," Nick said, trying to comfort her. He wished he was there so he could hold her and brush her hair. Comforting from a distance was difficult. "But you're a strong woman, just like your mother, and I know you have what it takes to see this through."

She swallowed the lump in her throat as his words buoyed her.

"How are you sisters holding up?"

"Better than I expected," she admitted, thinking how brave they had been earlier. "Mel has everything under control, as usual."

"And Cassie?"

"Believe it or not, we made it the entire afternoon without fighting."

"That's good to hear."

They sat on the phone in silence for another minute.

"I miss you." Eve broke the silence.

"Not as much as I miss you." Nick lay back on the bed. "I hope you don't mind, but I turned a light on in your house. The thought of your place being completely dark for an entire week was..."

"I don't mind." Eve smiled, realizing he'd done it because he missed her. "Well, it's late, and I need to get some rest. Tomorrow will be here before you know it. Good night."

"Night."

The next day, Eve went out to her father's workshop. She had spent some time walking through the place when she was there at Christmas, but she hadn't inspected it closely with everything going on.

She remembered fondly late afternoons and weekends out there with her dad while he worked on cars or radios or whatever he could find that was broken and needed a little tuning up. Opening the doors was like opening a window to the past. As she entered, she could almost see herself at ten or eleven, searching for a wrench. She had been at his side day and night, and anytime he was out there working, so was she.

She moved forward, examining the boxes of tools. Many of them were still in the same place where he'd left them before that awful day.

"I miss you." She smiled through blurry eyes as she grabbed a rag and wiped her hands.

As she walked around, reliving old memories, she rummaged through some boxes. Her father hated to throw anything away for fear he would need it later. More than once, Nancy had accused him of being a hoarder, to which he responded by telling her to mind her own business.

As Eve approached the workbench, she had the overwhelming feeling she wasn't alone, as if a piece of her father was still there, attached to the place he loved most.

"I can almost feel you here with me." She picked up an old picture of the two of them leaning against the hood of his Jeep. "God, that seems like a lifetime ago." She wiped away the dust from the glass. "I was happy then."

"Eve, dinner." Mel was calling to her from the house.

"Coming," she shouted, quickly drying her eyes.

As she turned to leave, she spotted a familiar black box on the counter. She took the rag and wiped the dust from the lid, then lifted it and found something entirely unexpected. There, glittering in the light of the dying sun, was a necklace.

Has this been here the entire time?

It was the only piece of jewelry her father had ever bought her, a gift when she turned eighteen. She removed it from the box and placed it around her neck.

Eve took turns with her sisters for the rest of the week as they monitored their mother's health. Cassie and Mel were glad to have a break, even if it was only for a few days. But as the week drew to a close, Eve felt more and more that she needed to be there, and not just temporarily.

By Sunday afternoon, Eve was back in Tennessee. Anxiously awaiting her arrival, Nick had been pacing the floors of the terminal, counting down the minutes. Seeing her walk up the ramp gave him a sense of relief, and as she found him with her eyes, he was there to greet her with a smile and open arms.

"God, I've missed you." He circled his arms around her.

"Not as much as I've missed you," she said, clinging to him.

"So, how was it?" He sensed things had been more difficult than she first imagined.

"Tough," she admitted. "But I got through it."

Nick drove home, and as they pulled into the drive, Eve was glad to be back on the farm.

He took her bags from the car and helped her inside.

"I kept a watch over the place, just like I promised." He set the suitcase near the steps. "Mostly, it was a quiet week."

"That's good." She let her hair down. "And work?"

"Busy," he replied. "Are you hungry? I could cook for you."

"That'd be lovely," she said, lying down on the sofa.

Nick grabbed a blanket and covered her up while he started dinner.

"Kathleen stopped by this morning," he told her from the kitchen. "I guess she thought you'd be home earlier. I told her I'd have you call her when you got back."

"That's nice," she mumbled. "I'll give her a ring after dinner."

"So how are Mel and Cassie? Any fireworks?"

"Actually, no."

Nick peeked around the corner. "Really?"

"Really," Eve said. "For the first time in my life, no. Believe it or not, Cassie was pleasant to me. In fact, she and I talked for a long time one night, just the two of us. I think this whole thing with Mom has really changed her."

"That's good to hear," he said as he put the chicken in the oven. He prepared dinner, and once it was ready, he went into the living room to get Eve, but somewhere between baking the chicken and steaming the vegetables, she had fallen asleep. Rather than wake her, he kissed her gently on the forehead, then pulled the cover around her so she wouldn't get cold. He ate alone and stayed there with her for a couple of hours. He found a dish and a lid and saved what was left of the meal, placing it in the fridge for later. Then, instead of going home, he grabbed a blanket and made himself comfortable in the chair.

When he woke, it was after six. Eve was still in the same spot from the night before. He went to her and woke her gently. It took a few minutes, but when she was good and awake, she smiled and thanked him for letting her sleep.

"I didn't have the heart to wake you." He brushed her hair with his hand. "You looked so peaceful."

She smiled. "I guess I was more tired than I thought." As she sat up and rubbed her eyes, she felt a great rumbling in her stomach. "But skipping supper wasn't the best idea."

"Why don't you get a shower while I make breakfast?" he offered.

A few minutes later, Eve descended the stairs in her robe. Her hair was still damp, but she wanted to eat before she finished getting ready for work.

"Thanks again for breakfast," she said as she sat down to eggs, toast, and bacon.

"Are you sure you have time?" He glanced at the clock on the wall. "It's almost eight."

"My first class isn't until ten, so…"

When Nick had rinsed the pans in the sink, he filled a glass with juice and joined Eve at the table.

"What are your plans for the day?" she asked as she sipped on orange juice.

"I've got to drive to Rutledge today and deliver some blankets and feed. Then I thought I'd swing by the market and grab something for dinner."

"Are we eating together tonight?"

"I wouldn't have it any other way," he said with a smile.

When breakfast was over, Eve went upstairs and put on a pair of blue slacks, the ones with the pinstripes, then added a white blouse before pulling her hair up into a bun. After grabbing her briefcase, she crossed the living room to where Nick was waiting to kiss her goodbye.

When Eve had departed, Nick set off for the house to begin his day.

CHAPTER 16

GUARDIAN ANGEL

Later that afternoon, Nick arrived home with ingredients to prepare a fish dinner. He'd caught several nice crappies while Eve was in Texas and had been keeping them in the freezer for a special occasion. Eve mentioned once how much she loved to eat fish from the lake, so he thought it would be a pleasant surprise.

Glancing at his watch, he realized it would be another couple of hours before Eve would be home, so he lay down on the couch to catch a nap in the meantime.

He had been asleep for almost an hour when a cry for help jolted him awake. He sat straight up and listened, wondering if what he had heard was real or part of the nightmare he'd been having. Any doubt quickly vanished when the call came a second time. Leaping from the couch, he rushed outside to see what was wrong. Setting his eyes down the hill, Nick was surprised to find Eve's car in the driveway. Automatically, he looked at his watch. *Curious*, he thought, not expecting her for at least another hour.

He turned his gaze south, where something stirring in the trees. Seconds later, another cry for help.

Having pinpointed the direction from which the cries came, Nick stepped off the porch and raced toward the woods. When he reached the other side, he stopped to catch his breath. Searching the area, he fixed on the pond and noticed a body facedown down in the water.

"Eve!"

Without hesitation, he bounded down the hill as fast as his legs would carry him through the tall grass. Reaching the dock, he dived in and retrieved her. When she was safely on dry ground, Nick rolled Eve onto her back and checked for a pulse. Nothing. Her face, an unnatural shade of purple, startled him, and for a moment, his mind was transported back to that night.

As he fought the demons of his past, he began CPR.

"You can't do this to me again," he said through gritted teeth as he turned his eyes skyward. He put his hands together and pressed them against Eve's chest, pulsing in regular intervals, stopping only to breathe air into her lungs. "Come back to me," he pleaded as tears fell freely from his eyes.

After what felt like minutes, he felt her body convulse beneath him. Nick rolled her onto her side and hit her back a few times as she expelled the water from her lungs.

"Nick?" Eve whispered as the life returned to her eyes.

A wave of relief washed over him. "Everything's going to be all right," he said shakily.

He held her close for a minute as his eyes scanned the area. Someone had alerted him to her presence, but who?

When the color had returned to Eve's face, Nick scooped her into his arms and carried her home. Once inside, he helped her up the stairs, where Eve changed out of her wet clothes. While she showered, Nick went downstairs to start a fire.

A half hour later, Eve emerged wearing a pair of white cotton shorts and a matching shirt.

Sensing her presence, Nick turned and found her with his eyes. Her skin, still damp from the shower, glistened in the firelight.

"How are you feeling?" he asked, steadying himself as he helped her to the couch.

"Better now," she answered as she tried to recall how she ended up in the water.

Nick grabbed a blanket and wrapped her in it, then asked if she wanted a drink.

"Something strong," she suggested, eager to forget.

After a quick search of the cabinets, Nick found the one with the alcohol. "Bourbon okay?" he asked, reaching for the bottle of Makers.

"Perfect," she replied, watching him intently. "The stiffer the better."

Nick's pulse jumped. He cast an eye in her direction, but she had looked away and was staring at the fire. After swallowing the lump in his throat, he poured two tumblers and added some ice, then joined her on the sofa.

"You gave me quite a scare today." He stared into the liquor.

"I know," she replied, feeling scolded. She sipped the bourbon and winced as the sting took hold of her. "I don't know what happened. I'm normally very sure-footed."

"I'm just glad someone alerted me," he said, tossing back the alcohol in a single shot.

"What do you mean?"

"Someone called out three or four times… loud enough to wake me from a nap."

Eve tried to concentrate, but her memory was still fuzzy.

"Maybe it was Andi," she offered, coming to the only logical conclusion. "She's the only other person I've ever seen down at the pond."

"It was a man's voice I heard."

"A man?" Eve asked, looking bewildered.

"Yes." Nick replayed the events in his head. "But I suppose it doesn't matter now. The main thing is I got to you in time, before…" His voice fell off as he considered what would have happened had he not reached her when he did. "For a second when you were lying there on the dock, all I could think of was that night." The hair on the back of his neck prickled.

Eve became instantly sober.

Nick got up to refill his cup, but no sooner had he made it to his feet than he felt Eve take hold of his arm. She pulled him back onto the sofa in one motion, then climbed on top and straddled him.

Before he could react, she pressed her lips firmly against his. This was a side of Eve he hadn't experienced before. Pulling back, Eve stared into his eyes, her pupils wide with desire. Taking the initiative, Nick reached for her shirt, lifted it over her head, and then made quick work of her shorts. In less than a second, he had them off. And as she stood naked before him, he admired her body in the firelight. Once he had removed his clothes, Nick returned to the sofa as Eve assumed control.

As the heat swirled around them, Nick wondered what had gotten into her. Perhaps her close brush with death had awakened something inside her that had been buried for a long time. But whatever it was, he was enjoying every second.

It was still dark outside when Nick opened his eyes. Unaware of the time, he could sense morning was not far off.

For a moment, the details of the previous night escaped him. Then he felt the warmth of her body against him, and in an instant, it all came flooding back. Still exhausted, he dozed off and woke again around eight. Putting on his pants and shirt, he descended to the kitchen to begin breakfast.

A few minutes later, Eve joined him.

"Morning," she said, appearing in the kitchen.

Nick looked up. "Yes, it is a good morning." He smiled. "Did you sleep well?"

"I think so," she replied, rubbing her head.

"Hangover?" he laughed.

"What?"

"From the bourbon?"

"That explains it," she said as she tried to clear the cobwebs. "I don't remember much when I drink the hard stuff."

He wondered, albeit briefly, if she was teasing him again. "What *do* you remember about last night?" he asked, his tone serious now.

"You pulled me out of the water... we talked a little... bourbon..."

"Anything else?"

She shook her head. "Did you stay over?"

"You're kidding. Tell me you're kidding," he said nervously.

A few seconds later, he breathed a sigh of relief as he watched the corners of her mouth curl into a smile.

"Whew!" He fell back against the counter. "You had me going for a minute."

"Sorry," she smiled, then leaned in and kissed him softly. "The truth is, I could never forget a night like that."

"Me either." He turned his attention back to the eggs. "What got into you, anyway?"

"What do you mean?"

"I don't know. It was like you were someone else."

"You didn't like it?" she asked.

"No. I did. I really did," he said, feeling suddenly flushed as his mind drifted back to the previous night.

"Then shut up and kiss me, you fool." She raised an eyebrow.

Nick did as she commanded, and as their lips met, he realized there was so much he still didn't know about her.

They ate their breakfast on the porch as they watched a doe and her baby drink from the creek. Now that Eve had rested, her mind remembered bits and pieces of what happened the previous evening. She remembered getting a phone call from Mel, who had provided an update on their mother's condition. The news had not been what she was hoping for, so she had taken a walk to clear her head. Having traversed the woods, she made her way to the pond, where she sat on the dock and stared out at the water. But when she was ready to return home, someone or something spooked her, and she fell back, hitting her head as she plunged into the water. The next thing she remembered was Nick hovering over her, looking white as a sheet.

"What's that?" Nick noticed the chain around Eve's neck for the first time, admiring the way the gold glittered in the morning light.

Eve snapped back to the present and looked down at the necklace. "Something I thought was gone forever," she said as she pulled it from beneath her shirt and showed it to Nick. "Isn't it beautiful? My dad bought it for me when I graduated high school."

Nick moved closer, inspecting the fragile piece of gold. "You're going to think I'm crazy," he said, easing back. "But I've seen that before."

"That's impossible." She tucked it beneath her shirt. "My father designed it himself."

"I don't doubt that, but I *have* seen it before," he insisted as he took another sip of juice.

Silence descended, and they both went back to watching the deer, who had moved farther downstream.

"Are you sure?" Eve asked again a minute later.

"Do you think I'm lying to you?" he asked amusingly.

"No, but..."

"You asked me once why I didn't purchase this place. Do you remember?"

She nodded, recalling the conversation. "You said the timing wasn't right."

"Exactly," he said. "The truth is the timing was more right than you know. I had already put in an offer and was in the process of having papers drawn up. My plan was to fix the place up and turn it into a rental property."

"Why didn't you say anything?"

Nick shrugged. "I didn't see the point in boring you with the details of something that didn't happen."

"And why bring it up now? Are you regretting not buying it?" She grinned.

"Of course not. Like I said, I was within a day or two of finalizing everything, but then something happened."

Eve leaned in, hanging on his every word.

"I had been out at the hardware store, buying lumber." The memory was still vivid. "When I returned home, I found a plain white envelope wedged in my front door. I've never been a superstitious person, but even I had to admit the timing was curious. Even after I had submitted the offer, I wondered if I had made the right decision. On the day I found the envelope, I had been asking for a sign that would point me in the right direction, and I got the message, loud and clear."

"Why? What did it say?" she asked, on the edge of her seat.

"Wait," he replied. "In big bold letters.

"That's it?" she asked, feeling slightly deflated.

Nick nodded. "And on the back was that symbol, the same one from your necklace."

"Do you still have it?" Eve asked, hoping to prove to him he had been wrong about the whole thing.

Nick shook his head.

Eve grumbled. "And you're certain it was this symbol?"

Nick looked at it again to appease her, but it only confirmed what he already knew to be true. "One hundred percent."

They talked for another hour, mostly about something Nick and Marjorie had been discussing over the phone the previous day, but Eve's mind was miles away.

AFTER THE SCARE Eve had given him at the pond, Nick knew he had to do everything in his power to protect her, and that got him thinking. One morning while she was at work, as he took inventory in his workshop, a new and exciting thought entered his head. It wasn't the first time he'd thought of asking Eve to marry him. In fact, since Christmas, he'd given it more thought. Only now was he convinced marrying her was the right choice.

Rather than spend the afternoon working as he had planned, Nick climbed in the truck and drove to town to scope out engagement rings. He parked across the street from Enix Jewelers and spent a few minutes working up the courage to go inside. He was not ashamed of the love he had for Eve but picking out a ring was an altogether different proposition.

Once he'd summoned the courage, he went inside and was greeted by a dark-haired woman who appeared behind the counter.

"Mornin'," she said kindly. "You're Nick Sullivan, aren't you?"

He looked up right away.

"Yes ma'am," he replied, wondering how she knew him.

"I'm Polly," she said. "My husband plays golf with your neighbor, Glenn."

Nick recalled Glenn mentioning once or twice in passing that he played golf.

Nick smiled politely as he shook her hand. Then, when the pleasantries were over, Polly asked if she could help him find anything.

"Engagement rings," he said nervously.

"Right this way," she said with a smile as she led him to the back of the store. "As you can see, we have quite a selection… everything from princess cut to oval and emerald… and in every size too." She paused, recognizing he was a fish out of water. "Why don't I let you look. If you have questions, just holler."

Nick thanked her and began perusing the rings. As he did, he thought back to when he had purchased Jessica's ring. Back then, he had been on a budget and a modest one at that, but when he'd spotted that marquise-cut diamond, he knew.

Scanning the selection, he found several he thought might be a good fit for Eve, but he couldn't decide.

"Can I see these two?" he asked Polly, pointing to a pair of princess-cut rings.

She opened the small door and carefully removed the rings,

handing them to Nick. "They're both beautiful rings, but if you want my opinion, this is the one I'd recommend." She selected the one with the diamonds around the bezel.

"Any reason?" He thought they were equally beautiful.

"It's one of a kind," she said, noting that her son, who also worked in the store, had made it himself. "Tell me, what's your girlfriend's name?"

"Eve," Nick said as he turned his attention to the one-of-a-kind ring. "Eve Gentry."

"You mean Professor Gentry?" Polly asked.

"You know Eve?"

"Not personally," she replied. "But I know of her. I have friends who are members of the Women of Service organization at LMU. We had a luncheon recently, and I remember some ladies talking about her."

"This is her first year teaching at the university," Nick explained. "She moved from Texas last summer." He wasn't sure why he added that last detail, but he relished the opportunity to talk about Eve to anyone who would listen.

"Well, from what I hear, she's a lovely young woman."

"Yes, she is," Nick said with a faint smile as his mind conjured an image of her.

"Should I get one of these rings ready?" Polly asked, sensing that Nick had already decided.

"Not today." He cleared his expression. "I'll need to give it a little more thought but thank you for the time... and the help."

Nick left the store and drove around for a while with the radio off, thinking. Eve was the one. He was convinced of that. But there was the situation with her mother, and he still didn't know if she was planning to teach beyond this year. Then of course there was the matter of his wife and daughter. He had convinced himself they wanted him to be happy, and so far, he had done an adequate job of keeping the demons at bay, but marriage was a huge step. And no matter how hard he tried, he couldn't shake the feeling that somewhere they were looking down on him, wondering why he had abandoned them.

Eventually, Nick found himself at the coffeehouse. He rarely sought advice, but when he did, Joyce was the only one he could trust.

The afternoon was slow, so he asked if she had time to talk outside. As they eased out to the table near the creek, Nick marveled at the beauty of the trees in spring.

"I think this place gets better every time I come here." He pulled out the chair for Joyce.

"I know what you mean." She let her gaze drift. "Nick are you sure everything is all right?" she asked, turning her attention to him.

"Everything is fine," he answered after a slight hesitation. "But I need your advice."

"I'm all ears." She leaned back.

"I'm thinking of asking Eve to marry me." Nick paused and waited for her reaction.

Joyce didn't respond right away. "I think that's a lovely idea," she said finally. "The two of you are well suited."

"And you don't think it's too soon?"

"Heavens no. Besides, when you find the right person, there's no such thing as too soon, only time wasted." She paused and waited for him to respond, but when he didn't, she continued. "What is it?"

"Do you think I'm being fair... to Jessica and Candice?" he asked, looking as though it pained him to do so.

Joyce drew in a long breath before answering. "I think you loved them very much." She reached for his hand. "Still do. That will never go away. But like I told you before, God gives us a heart that is capable of so much love. That means that you can go on loving them the way you always have and love Eve at the same time. You don't have to choose."

Nick thought about that for a long time before speaking again. "Thanks Joyce. I feel much better now." He paused. "You know, I was telling Eve a while back how much you remind me of my mother. I hope you don't mind my saying." He looked at her with a faint smile.

"I don't mind at all," she said, swelling with pride. "And if I've never told you, I consider you something of a son to me. I hope *you* don't mind."

Nick shook his head, his smile broadening.

"So when are you going to propose, and how?"

"I suppose I haven't gotten that far." He suddenly realized he'd neglected the most important part. "But I want to do it before the school year is over. That much I know."

Joyce laughed at that and remembered what it was like when she was last engaged—the butterflies, the excitement. How she envied Nick.

CHAPTER 17

PAYING RESPECTS

As April became May and the end of the school year was within sight, Nick wasn't the only one with a lot on his mind. Since spring break, Eve had become increasingly worried about her mother, to the point she was considering cutting the semester short so she could spend more time with her. She was also wrestling with whether to come back next semester, which had been weighing heavily on her. Then, of course, there was Andi and her situation. It had seemed to have resolved itself now that Eve and Liza had talked, but in the back of her mind, there was still something off about them she couldn't shake.

With so many thoughts swirling in her head, Eve found sleep difficult to come by. Rather than stare at the ceiling or try to count sheep, she swung her feet to the floor and went to the window. Nick's house, ordinarily dark at that time of night, was lit up like a Christmas tree. Eve's gaze drifted from the house to the barn, which was also aglow.

She glanced at the clock on the nightstand. Two thirty. On

impulse, she slipped into her sweatpants and a long-sleeved shirt, then found her tennis shoes and ventured out into the night. It was quiet there in the dark other than the sound of a lone screech owl high on the ridge. As an icy shiver washed over her, she crossed her arms and quickened her pace.

When she reached the barn, she found it empty. But the sound of the radio playing softly told her Nick had been there recently.

"Maybe he forgot to turn the lights out," she said to herself as she slid open the door to the workshop. Reaching for the light switch, something caught her eye. Curious, she moved forward a few steps and to her surprise found Nick lying on a blanket in the hay with a half-empty bottle of Jack Daniels beside him. When she was close enough to hear him breathing, she noticed his face was streaked with dried tears, and in his hand was a letter. Carefully, Eve worked it free.

Dear Jessica,

I am writing this letter because I don't know any other way to tell you I am trying to move forward with my life. Ever since the accident that took you and Candice from me, I've been standing in the darkness with no hope of finding the light. But last year, something truly extraordinary happened. Someone came into my life, and she has changed everything. I feel guilty for loving her the way I once loved you, and despite everyone telling me so, I must convince myself that is what you would have wanted for me.

Not a day goes by when I don't think of you and Candice and wonder what our lives would have been like if things hadn't gone so wrong. Candice would be driving now, and you and I would be worrying like we always did. Then I think of me and you and the nights we spent on the porch, swinging and talking, dreaming of the future, all beneath the stars of heaven. I hope those thoughts never leave me, that I never forget your beautiful face, your kind eyes, and the way you smiled at me.

I don't know what the future holds, but it feels good to get these words off my chest so I can make it through another day without you.

Until we meet again,

Nick

EVE PUT down the letter as she wiped tears from her eyes. On the surface, Nick appeared happy. She knew he loved her with as much of his heart as he could. But on the inside, he remained broken.

Still blurry-eyed, she left Nick and slipped back to her house.

The next morning, she woke earlier than usual and set out before sunrise. As she climbed into her car, she set her gaze up the hill. The lights were off in the barn and in the house, which told her that Nick had awakened and returned home after she left. With the words of the letter still fresh in her mind, she pulled out of the drive and headed north on the highway.

The Harrogate Cemetery was less than a mile from the university, so as Eve turned down Fulton Road, she drew in a breath to calm her nerves. She had never been fond of cemeteries, but as she turned onto the gravel road that led beneath the stone archway, she felt strangely calm. Easing beneath the giant oak at the center of the property, she brought the car to a halt as the sun appeared on the horizon. Exiting the car, she realized she didn't know where the graves were, but she chose a direction and went for it.

She hadn't gotten far when a voice called out to her from the top of the hill.

Eve turned around to find Liza moving quickly in her direction.

"What are you doing here?" Eve asked, shocked that anyone else would be there at that time of the morning.

"I come here to see my best friend almost every morning," she said sadly, then paused as she cleared her expression. "I prefer the morning, before the rest of the world is awake, don't you?"

Eve nodded. "Morning has always been my favorite time of day," she confessed, drawing in a breath of cool air. "I guess I have my dad to blame for that," she added with a smile. "How is Andi, by the way? She hasn't come around much lately. I hope I didn't do anything to scare her off."

"No. Nothing like that," Liza assured her. But you know teenagers. "They change their minds like the weather. So do you have a friend or family buried here?" she asked, watching as Eve studied the names on the headstones.

"Neither really," Eve said hopelessly. "The man that I'm dating, the one who lives in the house beside mine—"

"Nick, right?" Liza piped up, having recalled their conversation several weeks earlier.

"Yes, that's right. Anyway, his wife and daughter are buried here."

"How terrible," said Liza, putting a hand to her heart. "But he's so young."

"Car accident," Eve replied. "You probably read about it in the papers. It happened a few years back."

"You know," said Liza, now thinking back, "seems like I remember seeing something about it. That must be difficult for him."

"Yes, it is," Eve replied glumly. "But he's dealing with it."

"Is that why you're here?" Liza asked as they strolled along the path. "To see them?"

Eve felt awkward telling Liza why she'd come out there, but since she asked her directly, Eve saw no way of avoiding it. "I wanted to let them know how much he means to me," she said apprehensively. "You probably think I'm crazy. But it's important they understand I'm not trying to take him away from them." When Eve was finished, she paused, during which she doubted her own sanity.

Liza came to a stop near Jessica and Candice's headstones and turned to Eve. "Believe it or not, I don't think you're crazy at all. In fact, if they could talk to you, I imagine they'd be honored that you would try to set their minds at ease."

"Thank you," said Eve sincerely. "I feel much better. Well, this is it." She felt fortunate to find the graves without searching the entire lot.

"In that case, I'll leave you to it," said Liza. "It was nice seeing you again."

"You as well," Eve replied, letting her gaze linger on Liza as she eased down the hill.

When Liza was out of earshot, Eve placed a flower at the foot of the headstones, then spread out the blanket and sat down.

"Hello Jessica," she began after a long pause. "You don't know me, but my name is Eve Gentry. I'm a professor at the university, and I'm your husband's neighbor." She considered if what she was doing was completely mad. "I wanted to stop and pay my respects and let you know that Nick and I have become close over the past several months, and that I love him very much. The truth is, I think I love Nick more than anyone I've ever known." She stopped and considered that for several seconds before continuing. "More than anything though, I wanted to promise you I will do everything in my power to love and care for him. You see, my heart was recently broken by someone who I thought loved me. But when he said forever, he didn't really mean it. I'm not sure why I'm telling you all this, other than to say Nick will never forget you and Candice, and no matter what happens between us, I will never come between him and the memories he has of you."

Having said what she came to say, Eve stopped and exhaled. It took guts to do what she had done, and to have that off her chest was a tremendous relief. After a minute of silence, she gently folded the blanket and tucked it beneath her arm as she rose and walked back to the car. At the top of the hill, she turned around to look for Liza, but she was already gone. Thinking nothing of it, Eve drove to work and began her day.

CHAPTER 18

Change of Heart

For weeks, Nick had been thinking of asking Eve to marry him. He loved her, and he knew she loved him too, but there was still some doubt whether she was willing to make Tennessee her permanent home. Had her mother not been ill, the decision might have been a simple one, but considering the circumstances, her mind was anything but made up.

Over dinner one evening, Eve mentioned something to Nick about an end-of-the-year faculty party the university was hosting at the convention center in the Gap. It was to take place the week before school let out. Seeing an opportunity, the wheels in Nick's head began turning.

While Eve was at work one day, Nick returned to the jewelry store and was thankful to find Polly behind the counter when he entered. She remembered him having come in several weeks earlier, so she found the two rings he had been interested in and set them on the counter.

"And you say this one is one of a kind—nothing else like it?" he asked, wanting to make sure.

"Nowhere in the world," she said with confidence.

"Then I'll take it," he said, drawing in a deep breath.

"Nervous?" She handed it to her son for cleaning.

"As a matter of fact, I'm not sure I've ever been more nervous in my life," he admitted with a chuckle.

"First time getting married?"

Nick's smile, or what remained of it, quickly vanished. "No ma'am," he said, dropping his gaze.

"Well, hopefully this time will be different," she said optimistically, unaware of the details of his previous marriage.

After Nick paid for the ring, he examined it one last time before Polly placed it in a small black box and added a crimson bow.

Nick thanked Polly for her help as he eased toward the door.

"My pleasure," she said happily. "And let me know how things go, will you?"

"Will do." He left the store with his stomach in knots.

All the way home, the only thing he could think of was the look on Eve's face when she saw the ring. Then he imagined how she would react when he got down on one knee and asked her to be his wife. Would she say yes? Surely she would say yes. He had little doubt about that.

The last thing he wanted was for Eve to stumble across the ring. So when he got home, he hid it in a drawer he knew she would never look in. Once he was satisfied his secret was safe, he picked up the phone and dialed the number for Angelo's, making a reservation for the two of them following the faculty party. That's where he was planning to pop the question.

As he counted down the days until the big night, Nick noticed a shift in Eve's mood. She became increasingly distant to the point he worried if her mother's situation was starting to wear her down. They spent nearly every evening together, but her mind was always miles away. Nick tried to be sympathetic, realizing how difficult this must be for her, especially being so far from home. But with summer only weeks away, he hoped the time off would be just what the doctor ordered.

One evening when he'd summoned enough courage, Nick made a phone call he had been dreading ever since he'd decided to propose. He knew he didn't have to make the call, but the more he thought about it, the more he knew it was the right thing to do.

"It's me." Nick struggled to get the words out as a man picked up on the other end. Inside, Nick was a wreck, but he was doing a decent job of hiding it.

"Nick—good to hear from you, son. Is everything okay?" the man asked.

Nick hesitated, then finally answered. "Yes sir. Everything is fine. Listen, I wanted to call because… well… because…"

"You've met someone, haven't you?" Tony asked as if he could read his mind.

"How did you know?" Nick asked with a mix of surprise and relief.

"The tone of your voice," Tony said. "You sound markedly different from the last time we spoke, and there's only one thing I know of that can spark that kind of change—love."

Nick apologized, feeling suddenly guilty.

"Don't apologize. Every man needs love in his life, even you. Look, you're a good man, Nick. You loved my daughter with all your heart, and as her father, that's all I could have ever hoped for. What happened to Jessica… and to Candice…? I'll never get over it," he said, his tone dark. "And neither will you. But that doesn't mean we stop living. We must move forward. That's how the good Lord designed us."

He paused. "So, if you called to ask for my permission, the answer is yes. Go, live your life. Love and be loved. And if you ever need anything, you know Elizabeth and I are always here for you."

Nick found himself overtaken by emotion to the point words momentarily escaped him.

"Thank you, Tony... for everything," he said, not knowing if this was the last time they would talk.

"She must be pretty special," Tony noted after a few seconds of silence.

"Yes. She is." A slow smile worked its way across Nick's face.

When he hung up the phone, he felt as if the last pieces to the puzzle were falling into place.

ON THE NIGHT of the party, Eve wore the black strapless dress she'd been holding on to for a special occasion. Her black heels, the ones with the open toes, matched the dress to a T. She looked stunning, having let Kathleen do her hair and nails earlier that afternoon. Nick had told her he had a surprise and that they should drive separately. Eve didn't know what he had up his sleeve but agreed to meet him at the convention center around seven.

Eve arrived a few minutes early, but the place was already abuzz with activity. Entering through the double doors, she found dozens of her colleagues and their significant others crowded into the large room, mingling and enjoying conversation while they sampled hors d'oeuvres. Dozens of eyes fell upon her as she scanned the room in search of Nick. Seeing that he had not yet arrived, she made her way quietly to the bar, where she requested a glass of chardonnay. It didn't take long before Scott spotted her.

"Eve, you look… wow," he said as he looked her up and down. He knew she was out of his league, but he had to give it one last shot.

"Thanks," she said politely, but she reined it in before he got the wrong impression.

"So are you here with anyone?" he asked casually as he took a draw of his beer.

"Yes. My date will be here any minute," she answered quickly as the bartender handed her a glass of wine and a napkin.

Scott's courage was quickly crushed. "In that case, I'll leave you to it. Enjoy your evening."

Crisis averted, she thought as she took a drink.

"Let me guess—Scott?" came a familiar voice from behind her.

Eve turned to find a man in a tuxedo easing his way in her direction.

"Nick?" she asked, admiring his newly shaven face. "I almost didn't recognize you."

"I've been looking for an excuse to shave." He rubbed his chin. "Five years is a long time."

"Well, it must have taken someone special to convince you to part with something like that." She reached up and ran a hand across the smooth surface of his face.

Nick stared longingly into her eyes. "Very special." He dropped his voice to a whisper and leaned in for a kiss. "You look unbelievably beautiful."

"Thank you." She felt suddenly light-headed. "Drink?"

Nick ordered a bourbon on the rocks, then joined Eve as she introduced him to her colleagues. It surprised her how well he performed in conversation given his quiet nature, but he was witty and charming, presenting a side of himself Eve had never seen before.

When it was time for the ceremony to begin, Eve found their seats while Nick refilled their drinks. After the first award had been given out, Nick turned to Eve and asked if she thought she would receive something.

"Doubtful," she whispered. "Everyone else has been here a lot longer than me, so unless they give out an award for the least tenure, I don't think I have a chance."

After an hour, it came time to announce the Professor of the Year, the most distinguished award of the night. President James Dawson took the stage to a round of applause, and as he put on his reading glasses and adjusted the microphone, Nick was thinking about the dinner he had planned and the surprise that awaited Eve afterward. The more time passed, the more nervous he became, but he didn't let it show.

"Now to the moment you've all been waiting for," President Dawson announced, looking out at the crowd. "It gives me great pleasure to announce this year's Professor of the Year. As some of you may know, we had a young woman join our LMU family this past year all the way from the great state of Texas. Though she has only been with us a short time, her never-say-no attitude, tenacity, and teaching style have made a tremendous impact on the students and the faculty alike."

Connecting the dots, Nick turned his eyes to Eve, who looked on in stunned silence.

"This year's Professor of the Year award goes to Ms. Eve Gentry."

Everyone in the room stood and clapped as they turned their eyes upon her.

Overcome with emotion, she didn't know what to do.

"Go on," Nick urged, helping her to her feet.

Eve stood and made her way to the front as a wave of embarrassment washed over her.

"Wow, I… clearly wasn't expecting this," she said, nearly out of breath as she stepped up to the podium. She took a deep breath to steady her nerves, and as she scanned the crowd, her eyes settled on Nick. "Ever since I was a little girl, I had a dream of becoming a teacher. I worked hard in school, read every book I could get my hands on, and had a thirst for knowledge that has never gone away." She paused and cleared her throat. "Recently, I've had some setback in my life that tried to pull me away from my dreams, but when I was at my lowest, this university took a chance on me and offered me the opportunity of a lifetime, and for that I'll be eternally grateful." She paused as she reached up with her hand and wiped a tear from her eye. "My dad passed away a little over a year ago, but if he could be here tonight, he'd say Eve, this is what happens when talent meets hard work. So, Dad," she said, turning her eyes skyward, "this is for you."

At that, everyone in the room stood and applauded. Nick marveled at the way she shone in front of a room. She had that certain something that set her apart from everyone else, and it was then he realized that after all they had been through—the struggle, the loss, the heartache—that they were meant to be together.

As Eve was set to leave the stage, Dean Robbins walked up and addressed the crowd.

"Let's give Ms. Gentry another round of applause," she said, gesturing for Eve to remain on stage.

When the crowd returned to their seats, the dean continued.

"I think everyone would agree that having Ms. Gentry

around this year has been a breath of fresh air." Her eyes drifted to Eve, who was standing a few feet away. "That is why I will be sad to see her leave us at the end of the year."

A gasp went up from around the room. It took Nick a few seconds to comprehend, thinking that there must be some mistake.

"You see, Eve has decided to take some time away for personal reasons," Dean Robbins explained. "I realize I could have waited until Monday to make this announcement, but I wanted you to have the opportunity to thank her while we're all together."

At that moment, Eve felt her entire body go numb. When she'd told Dean Robbins hours earlier about her decision, she didn't know she would announce it to the world, especially before she told Nick. Now as she found him with her eyes, what she saw written on his face was a mix of confusion and disappointment.

When Dean Robbins was finished, Eve descended the stage and headed straight for the doors. To avoid unwanted attention, Nick waited a few seconds before he followed her. Once outside, he looked right, then left, and found her sitting on a bench with her head in her hands.

"When were you going to tell me?" he asked flatly, feeling as though the wind had been taken out of his sails.

"Tonight... at dinner," she confessed, unable to look him in the eye. "I didn't know she would announce it during the ceremony, honest." She paused. "I didn't even know I was getting an award."

"But what about waiting to see how the summer played out like we discussed?"

"I know, but Dean Robbins needed an answer, and I

couldn't keep her waiting any longer. I figured this was the best solution... for everyone."

"What about me?" He couldn't believe she had neglected to consider his feelings.

Eve dropped her head and turned away, and it was at that moment Nick realized the magical evening he had spent weeks carefully planning was crumbling before his very eyes.

"I don't suppose there's anything I could say to make you change your mind, is there?" he asked, still clinging to a shred of hope that the night could be salvaged.

She shook her head.

Nick sat in silence while he pondered his next move. "What about us?" he asked, arriving at the question she had feared above all others.

Eve found the courage to glance in his direction, but she did so behind blurry eyes. Sensing something terrible was coming, Nick swallowed the lump in his throat as he braced for the worst.

"I love you, Nick. You know that. But maybe it's a good idea if we slow things down for a while, just until I have some time to get my bearings."

Her words were like a dagger to his already breaking heart. After a while, with nothing else left to say, Nick rose and turned to leave.

"Where are you going?"

Nick didn't respond, just kept walking.

"What about dinner?" she asked, rising to her feet.

He stopped and raised his gaze to the restaurant across the street. The table he had requested, the one by the window with the candlelight and roses, was staring him in the face. His future, the one where he got his happily-ever-after, was feet away, and yet it was entirely out of reach. Without saying a word, Nick lowered his head and disappeared into the night.

NICK STAYED up most of the night staring at the ring, wondering how everything he'd planned so carefully had come unraveled so quickly. He should be with her, celebrating their engagement, and yet he was alone, miserable. Despite his love for Eve, regret crept into his mind, and he wondered if their chance encounter had been a blessing after all.

By dawn, his anger had not abated, so he left early and drove out of town, trying to escape the reality that his relationship with Eve might be over.

CHAPTER 19

THE ACCIDENT

When school ended, Eve cleaned out her office and said goodbye to her friends for the last time. She had been there less than a year but leaving was more complicated than she had imagined. Had her mind not been focused on home, surely, she would have teared up.

The next day, she boarded a plane for Texas. She left early and drove herself to the airport, not wanting to make things any harder on Nick than they already were. They hadn't spoken since the night of the party, and she wondered whether he still wanted anything to do with her after the way she treated him.

Eve stayed gone for almost a month, which gave her time to clear her head.

When she returned the Wednesday after Memorial Day, Nick was in his workshop.

"Hey stranger," she said softly, appearing in the doorway in a T-shirt and jeans.

Nick looked up at the sound of her voice and turned his

head slowly. For a moment, he thought he must be dreaming. "You're back," he said with controlled enthusiasm.

"I'm not disturbing you, am I?" She noticed he had let his beard grow out.

"Never." He eyed her intently as she stepped nervously inside the shop.

"Listen, I wanted to apologize… for the way we left things," she began. "I know I should have said something before now, but…" She dropped her gaze. "Anyway, I just wanted to tell you I'm sorry and I hope you can forgive me."

Nick had thought many times about this moment and what he might say to her. Deep down, he was still hurt, but at least the anger had subsided.

"I suppose we both acted foolishly," he admitted as he inched toward her. "It's just everything was going so well, and then… when I heard you had decided not to come back, I don't know. I felt like my entire world was spinning out of control and there was nothing I could do to stop it." He paused as the emotion from that night came flooding back. "But seeing you today makes me forget all those things. I want to be angry with you, God knows. But I can't." He moved closer. "The truth is, I love you." He reached up and brushed a strand of hair from in front of her eyes.

"And I love you," she said, daring to look at him.

"Then that's all that matters," he whispered. "Now that you're back, we can work through this."

Eve turned away. "I'm only here for a few days. I told Mel I'd be back at the beginning of the week to relieve her."

"Oh," said Nick as he put on a brave face.

"Mom is doing okay." Eve tried to redirect the conversation. "Her memory comes and goes, but at least she's in good spirits."

"That's good," he said, trying not to be insensitive. "I pray for her every night."

Something in the way he said it caught her off guard. "Thank you for that." She turned back to him. "I don't suppose I could interest you in dinner tonight?" She braced for outright rejection.

Nick thought about that for a few seconds before responding. "Sure, why not?"

That evening when Nick was finished in the shop, he washed up and descended the hill to Eve's place. This time he brought with him neither food nor drink, only himself.

Eve greeted him at the door and showed him into the living room, where she had a glass of wine waiting for him. "I know how you like the red," she said, handing it to him.

"Thanks." He tapped his glass against hers.

They ate dinner and talked, and although it was awkward at first, Nick and Eve found their rhythm once more, and by nine o'clock, they were laughing and enjoying one another's company as if nothing had happened. Between the wine and the excitement over having her back, Nick forgot about what she had done to him. But it was short-lived.

"Can I ask you something serious?" He set the wine on the table in front of him.

"Um, I suppose," she said, finishing her wine.

"Where do we go from here? Maybe this isn't the right time, but I feel as though we've been avoiding it since that night, and I'd like to get it out in the open."

That was a loaded question. Eve didn't respond right away as she had to consider her answer.

"I want to be with you," she said earnestly. "That hasn't changed. And I like it here. Actually, I love it here. Really, I do," she said, letting her gaze drift away from him. "And it will always hold a place in my heart…"

"But?"

"But it'll never be home, will it?"

"It could be," he replied, still clinging to a shred of hope as he gazed into her eyes.

"Nick, I—"

"Before you say anything, I want you to know I love you more than anything on this earth. You're the one who brought me out of the darkness, and for that I'm eternally grateful."

"And I love you." She paused. "But what if love isn't enough? What if, despite all we've overcome, a future together isn't in the cards for us?"

"I don't believe that," he said defiantly. "I won't believe that."

"Then what if I said I wanted you to come with me? Would you? Could you?"

"Move to Texas?" He sounded as though it was the most ridiculous thing anyone had ever asked him.

"Why not?"

Her question had caught him off guard. He had given a great deal of thought to asking her to marry him, had convinced himself it was the right thing to do, but at no time had he considered picking up and moving. What about his wife and daughter? Leaving them for two weeks had been hard enough but leaving for good was something he couldn't fathom.

"I don't know," he said. "My whole life is here."

"You mean your work?"

"That and—"

"Them?" she asked, cutting him short.

"Yes, them."

"But we could make a fresh start there, and there'd be plenty of work for you. Besides, you could keep your place here, and we could visit whenever we wanted." She paused, but despite her excitement, she could see he wasn't sold on the idea. "Look, I'm not asking you to forget about Jessica and Candice. I would never ask that of you. All I'm asking is for you to meet me halfway."

"I don't know if I can," he said miserably as his thoughts drifted once more to his family. "They've been with me for so long."

"You don't have to let them go," Eve said tenderly. "A part of them will remain with you always, the same way my dad will always be with me. But you have the rest of your life ahead of you, and so do I, and I need someone who can be there for me, not stuck in the past."

Nick weighed the pros and cons while he sat silently. When he'd reached a decision, he said, "I'm sorry, but I can't."

Eve shut her eyes, knowing her attempt had failed.

"Then that settles it," she said as she headed for the stairs.

"Where are you going?"

"To bed."

"Can't we talk this through?" he pleaded as she receded from sight.

"There's nothing left to talk about." She turned back to him as she reached the top. "We've both said all there is to say, and I fear more words would only make things harder than they already are."

"So you're saying it's over?"

"No, Nick." She forced a painful smile. "You are."

As she disappeared into the bedroom, Nick felt an aching inside him he hadn't felt since the night of the accident. All that time, and after all the care he'd taken to protect himself from moments like this, somehow, Eve had gotten in. Blaming himself, he left her house and returned home with his head hung in defeat.

AFTER THAT, Nick didn't see Eve for a long time. They spoke by phone once or twice, but even then, the conversation was brief and impersonal, and as the love they once shared withered away to nothing, Nick turned back to the only thing that brought him any comfort.

To keep from going mad, Nick poured himself into work, and in the evenings when the sun was low, he'd ride Shadow out to the lake to fish and think and drink. Sometimes while staring out at the water, he wondered if it had all been a dream —Eve, the romance they shared, and the spectacular fashion in which it had ended—and he'd reminisce about all the memories they had made along the way. He'd been so close to having everything he wanted, only to watch it slip through his fingers like sand through an hourglass.

Then, a few weeks before Labor Day, Eve returned to the farm. Her hair was longer, her skin dark from the summer sun. It was how Nick remembered her the first time they met, and if possible, she was more beautiful.

Nick wrestled with whether he should knock on her door, but he stayed by the window instead, hoping that she would forget about the last time they had spoken and come back to him. But after a few minutes, it was clear the love of his life had moved on.

Dejected, Nick withdrew to the couch and sat for a long time as the light from the sun faded. When he went returned to the window, the light was off, and her car was gone. That's when he knew it was truly over.

A month later, she returned for the last time. Nancy was living on borrowed time, and as the strain from her illness had taken its toll on Eve, the back-and-forth from Texas to Tennessee had left her exhausted. So she called up Sally and asked her to put the house on the market.

When Nick saw the sign being put in the yard, he waited until Sally was gone before descending the hill.

"Hey," she said, noticing him as he approached.

"Does this mean you're leaving for good?"

She nodded.

"How's your mom?" He redirected the conversation to avoid falling apart.

"Not good," she said. "The doctors say it'll be any day now. I just came back to sign the papers to get this place on the market. I leave for home tomorrow morning."

"And there's nothing I can say to change your mind?"

She shook her head.

"I had to ask," he said, forcing a smile.

"I don't suppose you've changed your mind about leaving, have you?"

Nick dropped his gaze and shook his head. "Eve, I—"

"You don't have to explain. I understand." She chuckled. "It's funny. I suppose I was right after all, wasn't I?"

"About what?"

"Sometimes love isn't enough to bridge the distance between two hearts."

Nick dropped his head in defeat.

Eve leaned in and kissed him on the cheek, and it was then she smelled the alcohol on his breath. "Well, I've got some things to take care of, but it was nice seeing you again."

"Yeah. You too," he said, his heart breaking.

THAT EVENING he sat in the rocker and stared at Eve's house for a long time. When the sun faded and the darkness swallowed up the land, he went inside and wept. The woman he loved was leaving, never to return, and he couldn't help but feel as if he'd made the biggest mistake of his life.

While Eve packed up her belongings, steady rain fell. Hearing the unmistakable sound of raindrops on the tin roof reminded her of happier times when she and Nick had been so in love. As she reminisced, a knock fell upon the door. Hoping Nick had reconsidered, she took in a breath and crossed the floor, but who she found waiting for her on the other side was unexpected.

"Andi, what are you doing here?" Eve showed her in.

"Are you leaving?" she asked, her smile fading as she spotted the stack of boxes.

"Yes. I'm afraid so," she answered solemnly.

"Why? I thought you were happy here?" She paused. "And what about Nick?"

Eve let out a breath. "It's complicated," she replied as she taped up the last box.

"Don't you love him anymore?"

"I do," she said. "More than I've ever loved anyone in my life, but—"

"Then I don't understand," she said, looking downtrodden.

"These are adult matters we're talking about," said Eve. "Perhaps one day when you're older you will understand. But this doesn't mean you and I can't still be friends." She tried to lighten the mood. "You can call me anytime, or you could write."

Andi forced a smile. But it was short-lived. "Yeah," she said half-heartedly.

"Tell your mom I said goodbye, will you?"

Andi nodded.

Just then, the roar of a vehicle descending the drive caught their attention.

"Oh no," said Eve.

"What's the matter?" Andi asked.

"No time to explain." Eve grabbed her keys as she headed for the door.

But Andi was quick to react, and in less than a second, she was on Eve's heels.

They got in the car and followed Nick as the rain intensified. As Eve approached the hairpin turn, she saw skid marks on the road ahead. Then, as she brought the car to a stop, she glimpsed the unmistakable glow of taillights down the hill.

"What happened?" Eve exited the car. "Oh my God." She jumped from the car. "Stay here," she told Andi as she descended the hill.

Eve shouted for Nick, but amid the thunder and rain and the sound of her own heart beating out of her chest, she heard nothing.

When she made it to the driver's-side door, she peered inside. But it was too dark to see anything. Reaching for her cell, she turned on the flashlight and shined it inside. That's when she saw his face covered in blood, and for a moment, the entire world stopped.

"Is he okay?" she heard Andi say from the street.

The sound of the girl's voice brought Eve out of her trance.

"Go across the street and call 911," Eve instructed.

While Andi went in search of help, Eve worked the door open. After freeing Nick from the seat belt, she tugged at him until he was out of the truck. Using her jacket, she shielded him from the rain as the sound of sirens sounded off in the distance.

"Stay with me," she pleaded, holding his head in her lap as tears welled in her eyes. Just then, just as hope faded, something stirred in the darkness. Eve looked up and found a familiar face staring back at her.

"Liza," she whispered, hardly audible. "How—?"

Liza swiveled her gaze from Eve to Nick, and when she did, Eve felt a sense of calm overtake her.

"May I?" Liza asked softly, kneeling beside Nick as the rain continued to pour.

Eve backed away as Liza put a hand beneath Nick's head. For a moment, Eve felt as though she were caught in a dream. She watched silently as Liza lifted his head and held it in her lap, whispering something to him that Eve could not make out.

As she inched back, Eve's hand brushed against an object with hard edges. She took hold of it and held it up in the light. It was a picture of Nick's family, taken shortly before they died. And it was at that moment Eve realized she had never seen a picture of Jessica or Candice, other than the small photo of Candice Nick kept in his truck from when she was four. Seeing them now, illuminated by the flashes of lightning, her blood ran cold.

Gripped by unimaginable fear, Eve shifted her gaze from the picture to Liza and then to Andi, who had returned and was kneeling beside her mother. As Liza continued to comfort Nick, Andi reached down and wiped away the blood from his mouth. Eve wanted to say something—a million somethings— but found herself frozen to the spot, incapable of words.

Just then the roar of sirens filled the air as the ambulance arrived. When Eve turned back, both Liza and Andi had retreated into the darkness. As the paramedics descended the hill, Eve searched the dark, but in vain.

~

WHEN NICK WOKE the next morning, he was staring up at a blank ceiling. He tried to move, but every part of him ached. After a minute, he worked the lids of his eyes open and quietly scanned the room, his eyes settling on Eve, who was curled up in the chair beneath a blanket. Even in the dim light, he could tell her hair was damp.

He called out to her, but his voice was weak as if he hadn't spoken in a long time.

Even so, Eve stirred at its sound. "Nick?" She threw aside the blanket and reached for him. "Thank God you're all right." She kissed his hand, then laid her head gently against his chest.

"Where am I?" he asked, fighting confusion.

"The hospital," she said. "You had an accident."

"Accident?"

"But you're going to be okay. Everything is going to be okay now." She forced a smile.

Nick lay there for a few more minutes as the nurses came in to check on him. Once he'd cleared the cobwebs, he sat up in bed and noticed his left arm was in a sling.

"I was having the strangest dream," he told Eve when they were alone. "Jessica and Candice were there... and so were you," he said, the memory still vivid.

Eve listened in silence.

"I was standing at the edge of a dark lake, and in the distance, I could see a bright light. I wanted to go toward the light, but something kept pulling me back. It was then I realized I wasn't alone. That's when I saw them. I asked them if I had died and gone to heaven, but they just smiled and told me how much they loved me and that it was all going to be okay. I know it sounds crazy, but it was so real."

"Maybe it was real."

Nick thought about that for a minute before responding. "Anyway, I feel different today."

"How so?"

"I don't know, but while I was asleep, all I remember is a voice telling me it's time to let go."

"Was it Jessica?"

Nick tried to recall, but no matter how hard he tried, he couldn't remember. "Do you think it's too late for us?" he asked, squeezing her hand.

Eve looked up and shook her head. "Never too late," she said, then kissed him.

CHAPTER 20

TEXAS OR TENNESSEE

After spending two days in the hospital, Nick was released and returned home to heal on his own. He had some bumps and bruises and a broken left arm, but he was going to survive. He was lucky though, and he knew it.

Eve did her best to take care of him and nurse him back to health, but a few days later, she received a call from Mel with bad news. Nancy's body was shutting down. Eve booked the next flight out. A couple of hours before she had to leave for the airport, there was an important stop she wanted to make.

At the end of Brantley Road, tucked away in a dark hollow, sat Andi and Liza's home. Eve parked the car at the spot where the gravel met dirt and approached the house. Skeptical she would find either of them there, it surprised her when Andi answered the door.

"I was wondering when you'd show up," she said, easing out onto the porch. Her hair was up in a ponytail, which Eve noticed right away. "I assume since you didn't come by sooner that Nick is okay."

"He's a little banged up, but he'll survive." Eve paused as she cleared her expression. "I wanted to thank you... and your mom."

"For what?" Andi asked as she stepped off the porch.

"For what you did that night," Eve answered, strolling alongside her down the dirt path.

"What did we do?" she asked coyly, keeping her eyes ahead, hands laced behind her.

Eve gave a look as if to prod her, but it was clear she was keeping quiet after a few seconds. "So, what now?" Eve changed the subject.

Andi shrugged. "I suppose I could ask you the same thing," she replied, daring a glance in her direction.

"My mother is dying," Eve said. "My sister called this morning and said she likely won't make it through the night. I'm catching a plane in a couple of hours. I only hope it's not too late."

Andi glanced at her watch. "You'll make it," she said, almost prophetically, then paused. "What about after?" she asked as they continued their walk.

"Don't know," Eve said, having given little thought to what she would do once her mother was gone. "School starts in a couple of weeks, so it's likely too late to get my job back." She laughed. "I suppose I should have listened to Nick and waited."

"Might be a good time to travel," Andi suggested. "You know, see the sights. I hear Arizona is nice this time of year."

Eve smiled, thinking of how she'd always wanted to see the Grand Canyon. "Maybe you're right." They came to the end of the road and stopped. "Will I ever see you again?" Eve asked, arriving at the question that had been burning in her mind since that night in the rain.

Andi shrugged as her eyes drifted to the heavens. "Only

God knows what the future holds," she said cryptically. "But perhaps somewhere down the road we'll run into one another again."

"I'd like that," said Eve sincerely.

"So would I," said Andi. "You're a good person." She swiveled her chestnut gaze to Eve. "And you're perfect for my da—I mean Nick. Just promise me one thing."

"Anything," said Eve.

"Come back and visit sometime. I'd love to show you the house when it's finished," she said, looking up the hill to the old Ousley place.

"You have my word," she said, then hugged Andi. "Thank you for everything," she whispered as she held on to her.

"You're welcome," she whispered back, and when she withdrew, there were tears in both their eyes. "Oh, I almost forgot." Andi ran back to the house and returned a minute later, holding a small wooden box with a butterfly painted on the lid. "When he's ready, give this to him, would you?"

"What is it?"

"He'll know what it is. Just promise not to open it, okay?"

"I promise," said Eve, giving it a little shake. She glanced at her watch, then let out a sigh. "I hate to run, but I've got a plane to catch, so…"

"Then you'd better get to it," said Andi.

When they parted, Andi walked home, and Eve returned to her car.

"By the way," Andi said as she reached the porch, "he says he's very proud of you."

Eve stopped dead in her tracks as the hair on the back of her neck prickled. Turning around, Eve wanted to ask a question, but it was too late. Andi was gone. Afterward, Eve sat in the car for a long time and cried as she looked down at the necklace her father had given her. And it was then she felt it, his presence, and she realized he had been right there with her all along.

By the time she made it back to Nick's, Eve only had a short while before she had to leave. But before she finished packing, she gave him the box like Andi had requested. He stared at it for a long time before he said anything.

"Where did you get this?" he asked, summoning the courage to speak.

"A friend wanted you to have it," she said, sitting beside him on the couch.

"Andi?" he asked, looking at her.

"Something like that," Eve said with a wry smile, but Nick paid little attention.

He ran his finger across the butterfly on the lid and thought back. "I haven't seen this in a very long time," he said as he fought a tidal wave of emotion. Lifting the lid, he peered inside, and what he found brought tears to his eyes.

"What is it?" Eve inquired.

Nick reached into the box and took out a pair of matching butterfly barrettes he had given to Jessica and Candice the day Candice started kindergarten. They were wearing them the night of the accident.

"I never thought I'd see these again," he said as he looked at them through blurry eyes. "Thank you." He pulled Eve close to him as he kissed her forehead. "You don't know what these mean to me."

"Tell me something," she requested as they parted. "Do you ever get the feeling they're still here with you?"

Nick smiled and said, "Sometimes. Occasionally I think I

see something, or I'll pass someone on the road that looks just like them, and I have to remind myself they're gone. I know it's only my imagination, but for a second it feels real." He paused and let his smile fade. "That probably sounds ridiculous," he added with a chuckle.

"No," she said tenderly. "I thought I saw my father once," she continued, her tone serious. "A few weeks after he died, I was in my room. Mom had already drifted off to sleep, and the house was quiet. I had been crying, so I went to the window to let in some fresh air, and when I did, I noticed a light on in my dad's workshop. I had been out there earlier in the day, but I could have sworn I turned out the light. Anyway, as I was about to go back to bed, I thought I saw someone moving inside. Just like you, I'm sure it was my imagination, but for a second I thought it was him." Eve paused as a chill washed over her. "Even now I get goose bumps thinking about it." She cast her gaze to Nick, who was smiling at her amusingly.

"Over the years, I've learned never to discount anything. Who knows, maybe there is life after death," he mused aloud.

"Does that mean you've changed your mind... about the possibility of ghosts?"

"I wouldn't go that far," he said as he leaned back and grinned. "But I think there are things that go beyond human understanding, and sometimes if the love is powerful enough, there are bonds that can never be broken." Nick left it at that, which was good enough for Eve.

WHEN EVE LANDED AT DFW, she wasn't alone. Despite the doctor telling him to rest, Nick wanted to be there for her.

Nick tried to keep the conversation light as they made their way to the hospital, but both knew what lay ahead. This would be the hardest thing Eve would ever have to go through. As Nick knew all too well, losing one parent was bad enough, but once they were both gone, the indescribable loneliness that followed was perhaps the worst part.

By the time they made it to the hospital, darkness had fallen. Cassie and Mel were already there, along with their families, who sat somberly in the waiting room. Eve joined her sisters while Nick waited outside with the others.

Quietly, Eve sat at her mother's bedside and watched helplessly as she slipped into a coma. The doctor came in a few minutes later and told them it was only a matter of time before her body would shut down completely. Despite wanting to tell her mother to hold on and fight, Eve realized this was the end.

Mel and Cassie were both in tears as the doctor removed the breathing tube. Each took turns saying their last goodbyes.

As they stood there, none of them knowing quite what to do, Eve thought about what her mom had said to her at Christmas—how she wanted them to be happy and love one another. Now the three of them were all that remained of their family, brought together by tragedy, their differences stripped away. The moment was too poignant to ignore.

Nancy Gentry held on for another minute. Then, when her body could fight no more, she gave up and left this world to be with her beloved Frank.

That first night was the hardest for Eve, but Nick was there and held her in his arms as she cried herself to sleep. The funeral was a few days later, and nearly everyone in the town of Athens attended. The turnout made Eve realize how many people her mother had touched throughout her life, and she felt guilty for not trying to work things out with her mom sooner. Still, she found some solace because they had reconciled, and it was in the days since that she realized just how much her mother loved her.

Eve and Nick stayed in Texas for another two weeks before going back to Tennessee. When they returned, Sally phoned Eve to let her know someone had put in an offer on the house. It was the full asking price. With most of her things in storage, Eve stayed at Nick's place until they figured out their next move.

"Having second thoughts?" Nick asked as they sat out on the porch late in the evening. His eyes were on Eve, who was staring down the hill at the farmhouse.

"You know me too well," she said glumly. "I only wish I'd listened to you in the first place, then maybe I'd still be teaching, and I wouldn't have put my house up for sale."

"Things happen for a reason," he said with a smile. "Besides, you were only doing what you thought was best. And if you don't want to sell the house, you can always back out. People change their mind all the time."

"I wouldn't want to do that to the buyer. I remember how excited I was when I saw this place, and I can't imagine pulling the rug out from under someone at the last minute." Eve paused as she tried to push it out of her mind. "Don't you think it's odd though that Sally doesn't know who put in the offer?" she asked, returning to a question that had been bothering her for a while.

Nick nodded but reassured her there was nothing to worry about.

Two weeks later, Eve closed on the house. The buyer had already signed the papers the day before, and when Eve was finished with her portion of the documents, looked at Sally and said, "Now that it's over, can you tell me who bought the house?"

Sally only smiled as she stacked the papers and put them in her briefcase.

"The buyer has requested you meet him at the house," she said, laying a hand on her shoulder.

Eve seemed puzzled by this request, but given her curiosity, she went along with it. When she pulled up and parked in front of the house, she noticed the lights were off, and there was no car in the drive. For a moment, she wondered if anyone was inside. Then she saw someone move within.

As she got out of the car, she thought back on all the memories made over the past year. Fighting emotion, she ascended the porch, and as she did, she gazed up the hill at Nick's place and remembered that first day when she and Kathleen speculated who her new neighbor would be. Then she thought about the first time she had seen him in the work-shop, the first time he kissed her beneath the shade of the oak, and the first time they made love.

Swallowing the lump in her throat, Eve collected her thoughts and knocked on the door.

"It's open," she heard a voice say. It belonged to a man.

Eve pushed open the door to find the room cast in the warm glow of candlelight. Shocked and confused, she didn't know what to make of the scene, but just then, Nick appeared.

"Surprise," he said sweetly, crossing the floor to where she stood.

"I... don't understand," she said, still fighting confusion.

"I couldn't let this place go to someone else." He took her by the hands. "It wouldn't have been right. So I bought it."

"You? But how?"

"I had some money saved up, and I know we haven't

decided yet where we want to live, but there are so many wonderful memories here and I'd like to hold on to those for a while. You're not mad, are you?" He paused, judging her reaction.

"No," Eve said, shaking her head as tears welled in her eyes. "I'm not mad at all. In fact, I'm thrilled." She put her arms around his neck and hugged him tightly. He had given her the greatest gift of her life, and she loved him even more than she did before.

"Good." Nick took a step back. "In that case, I have something I want to ask you," he continued, dropping to one knee. He reached into his pocket and pulled out the box with the ring.

Eve's hands went to her mouth as new tears fell.

"Eve Gentry," he began, raising his gaze to hers. "A year ago, you came into my life and led me out of the darkness. Words can't express the way I feel about you but know that I love you with all my heart and want to spend the rest of my life with you by my side." He paused and lifted the lid, revealing the diamond ring. "Eve Harper Gentry, will you marry me?"

"Yes," she said. "A million times yes." She pulled Nick to his feet and kissed him.

It was the moment they had both been waiting for, and after all they had been through—the pain, suffering, and loss— heaven was finally shining down on them.

That evening, as a warm sun set in a sky of pink and purple, Nick Sullivan and Eve Gentry left the darkness behind and stepped into the light. As they stood on the porch, gazing off at the sunset, two Monarchs danced effortlessly on the back of the evening breeze.

They watched in silence until the butterflies were gone, then set their eyes upon one another once more.

"So, what'll it be—Texas or Tennessee?" Nick asked as he held her in his arms.

Eve thought for a few seconds before answering, then looked into his eyes and said, "I was thinking Arizona. I hear it's nice this time of year."

END

AFTERWORD

Thank you for reading Between Your Heart and Mine. If you enjoyed the book, please leave an honest review. In the meantime, please check out my other work at:

www.buckturner.com

Printed in Great Britain
by Amazon

24111333R00131